Binge

FICTION BY DOUGLAS COUPLAND

Worst. Person. Ever.
Player One
Generation A
The Gum Thief
JPod
Eleanor Rigby
Hey Nostradamus!
All Families Are Psychotic
Miss Wyoming
Girlfriend in a Coma
Microserfs
Life After God
Shampoo Planet
Generation X

Binge

60 stories to make
your brain feel different

Douglas Coupland

Random House Canada

PUBLISHED BY RANDOM HOUSE CANADA

www.penguinrandomhouse.ca

Random House Canada and colophon are registered trademarks.

LIBRARY AND ARCHIVES CANADA CATALOGUING IN PUBLICATION

Title: Binge : 61 stories to make your head feel different / Douglas Coupland.
Names: Coupland, Douglas, author.
Description: Short stories.
Identifiers: Canadiana (print) 20210147938 | Canadiana (ebook) 20210147962 |
    ISBN 9781039000520 (hardcover) | ISBN 9781039000537 (EPUB)
Classification: LCC PS8555.O8253 B56 2021 | DDC C813/.54—dc23

Text design: Leah Springate
Jacket design: Douglas Coupland
Image credits: Paul Natkin / Contributor / Getty Images

Printed in the United States of America

10 9 8 7 6 5 4 3 2 1

Penguin
Random House
RANDOM HOUSE CANADA

This book is dedicated to both Siri who lives in my Mac and Siri, my niece (Norwegian goddess of laughter), who was in junior high school when Siri became a thing. Imagine what that must have been like. She's one of the most delightful talkers and texters I know.

Contents

01

Alexa

PEOPLE ASK ME THINGS like where I parked my car, say, 477 days ago and I'm immediately able to tell them it was slot 173 on the third level of the Walgreens parkade and that it cost $1.50 and there was a dark-blue Subaru wagon on my left with a stuffed Garfield doll wearing sunglasses on the dashboard. I don't need an app to remember this. I'm one of a few people on earth who remembers every single thing they've ever seen. Everything. If you think this is bullshit, let me ask you a question: Have you ever been in a car accident or something that, when you remember it later, feels like it took ten minutes instead of ten seconds? Like it happened in slow motion? I bet you have. This is because your brain filmed it twice—once with your regular memory and at the same time with your fight-or-flight memory camera. Most people's fight-or-flight memory only kicks in when they're experiencing a traumatic event. Mine has been filming non-stop for my entire life.

I remember the license plate number of the car parked in front of my mom's when she dropped me off for school on the morning of November 14 in third grade: MDL5588.

1

I remember what my teacher was wearing that day: green dress; bandage on her left hand. I remember the questions on the geography test (of course I scored 100 percent). My parents sent me to school only because they didn't want me to be socially maladapted, not because I was learning anything new there.

Once doctors figured out what was going on inside my head, any chance at me having a normal life was over. They'd ask me to memorize pi to five thousand digits, but what they called memorization is, to me, simply looking at something and describing it afterward. Tying my shoelace is more work for me than recalling your American Express card number five years after you showed it to me over drinks on that night when there was a waning crescent moon setting directly into the skimming net beside the swimming pool heater that was set at 90 degrees Fahrenheit.

Tell me how you get to work each morning. Obviously you know your route. It's not a big deal, and if you told it to me fifty times, it would be the same every time. Why wouldn't it? That's how my memory works; it's no different than you telling me your daily route to the office.

Languages are easy . . . we all learn to speak them without even being aware of it. I learned Navajo in a week. I now speak twelve, but it's not much fun being a freak when you get right down to it. For instance, it doesn't help my dating life. Once a person learns about my condition, they immediately assume I'm "monitoring" them and they get paranoid. Like they're so interesting! People are so similar they could be identical.

The other thing about remembering everything is the sad knowledge that almost all of what's in my head is unnecessary junk. To get through life, you barely need to remember anything, let alone every single word of a five-thousand-word article on the reintroduction of protein into the post-WWII Japanese diet or all of the end credits for all of the *Star Wars* movies.

When Google came along, I thought finally everyone would feel what it's like to be me. But all it did was make people remember less. (Having said that, I have noticed that when people look something up on Wikipedia, they tend to actually remember it; I'm guessing that a certain kind of curiosity triggers your brain to secrete chemicals that cement your newly learned facts in your brain.)

I actually went a bit crazy in my late twenties and started avoiding any situation where I'd see words: not just books and magazines and street signage, but words in the online world as well. Imagine remembering every scattershot piece of junk you've ever seen on even the most basic trip down the rabbit hole—you'd go mad. I thought the cure for my soul was to focus on nature: plants and animals and soil. But without words and language to occupy me, my brain started overcompensating. Soon the landscapes and buildings around me started to explode into astonishing levels of detail. Noticing insects everywhere was the worst of it. And stains. And flaws and bruises. Scratches. The faces and animals I saw in the clouds.

I reached a crisis point when I was walking past a souvenir store near the weekend flea market. I turned my head and saw someone revolving one of those racks full of miniature license plates with kids' names on them. I did not want to see this.

ABIGAIL	ADDISON
AIDEN	ALEXA
ALEXANDER	ALEXIS
ALLISON	ALYSSA
AMELIA	ANGEL
ANDREW	ANNA
ANTHONY	ASHLEY
AUBREY	AVA
AVERY	BELLA
BRANDON	BRAYDEN
BRIANNA	BROOKLYN
CARTER	CHARLOTTE
CHLOE	CHRISTIAN
CHRISTOPHER	CONNOR
DANIEL	DAVID
DYLAN	ELIJAH
ELIZABETH	ELLA
EMILY	EMMA
ETHAN	EVAN
EVELYN	GABRIEL
GAVIN	GRACE
HAILEY	ISABELLA
ISAAC	ISAIAH
JACK	JACKSON
JACOB	JAMES

JAYDEN	JOHN
JONATHAN	JORDAN
JOSEPH	JOSHUA
JUSTIN	KAYLA
KAYLEE	LANDON
LAYLA	LEAH
LIAM	LILY
LOGAN	LUCAS
LUKE	MADISON
MAKAYLA	MASON
MATTHEW	MIA
MICHAEL	NATHAN
NATALIE	NEVAEH
NICHOLAS	NOAH
OLIVIA	OWEN
RILEY	RYAN
SAMANTHA	SAMUEL
SARAH	SAVANNAH
SOFIA	SOPHIA
TAYLOR	TYLER
VICTORIA	WILLIAM
ZOE	ZOEY

Something snapped inside me. I ran to the park across the street and sat down on a bench and cried. I hate feeling sorry for myself.

A woman who ran one of the flea market booths had noticed me take off. She followed me to make sure I was okay. She was sixty-eight years old (24,843 days old, actually), and she really seemed to care about me. Maybe she was just looking to distract me, but she asked if she could draw me. Sure, I said, and I went with her back to her booth and sat in her green folding beach chair. For an hour or so, she drew me with charcoal, and all the while she asked me about myself in a way nobody ever had. When she was done, she showed me my portrait. It didn't pander. She then asked me to switch places and draw her. Which I did.

And that's the day I became an artist. Nobody blames an artist for noticing stuff.

02

Radiation

TWO YEARS AGO THIS APRIL, I held my fortieth birthday brunch on the back deck. It was sunny and just warm
enough outside that if all my friends wore down vests and
my wife, Lucy, supplied a few blankets, we could pretend
the weather was warmer than it really was. (By April you
are basically desperate for some heat and light.) There
were eight of us, all around the same age, as well as a few
kids, who we parked in the TV room. It was a good gather-
ing and I was feeling grown-up in a way I find rare: *Look at
me! I'm having a cosmopolitan fortieth birthday on the
deck of a home that has an $800,000 mortgage. I'm truly an
adult now!*

A quick note about Lucy. Everything my wife does has to
be perfect, like a traditionally brined and roasted turkey at
Thanksgiving. Also, she has no internal coping mechanism
for when things go wrong.

Since all of us were more or less the same age, we spent
some time discussing the meaning of turning forty. Nathan,
our official web-savvy friend, said, "Craig, if Lucy gets hit
by a bus, you'll be way too old to find a date. You'll need to

check out the Azerbaijani bride websites. You'd be amazed what's out there."

Lucy said, "Nathan, don't put ideas in his head."

"Seriously, Lucy, we should check one out later. We'll all choose your replacement."

"You scallywag."

Claire, our official witty/cynical friend, then added, "Craig, you'll have to be on the lookout for gold diggers. The smart ones hang around vintage car events. Let's be honest, if a woman compliments a forty-something straight guy on the color of his car, in his head he's already moving her into a love nest." She took a sip of her beer. "I feel like I should be charging you all actual money for that piece of advice."

Our friend Noah would normally have been all over this, but he wasn't. Lucy was the first to notice. "Noah, you look a bit peaky today—the kids keeping you up at night?"

Noah glanced at his wife, Jeannie, and then at all of us. "Well . . . we've been meaning to tell you this, but no time seemed like the right time, I guess. I'll just say it: I've been getting radiation treatment for thyroid cancer. They say I'm going to be okay—but I have to apply this pale-green makeup to my throat so it won't look sunburned red, and it makes my flesh look like rubber."

Lucy was horrified. "Noah, I'm so sorry. I—"

"No, don't be. Jeannie and I are at peace with things. We have every confidence I'll make it through okay."

Silence.

Noah finally said, "I shouldn't have dropped that on all of you. Tom, tell us a joke to change the tone here."

Tom, our slightly-on-the-spectrum scientific friend, obliged. "A New Caledonian crow, a Great Pacific octopus and Prince Harry walk into a bar—"

And then that's when the gods shone down. Lucy glanced up at the sky and said, "Oh look! It's a bald eagle!"

A bald eagle. In Alaska I guess they're common, but down here they're pretty rare. Mother Nature had decided to change the subject.

"I grew up thinking they were almost extinct," said Claire.

"I think they almost were," said Tom. "Back then they were probably grinding them up to make paper towels or automotive paint or something."

"It's so majestic!" said Jeannie. "It sounds so corny, but look at it!"

And it was indeed majestic.

We stood on the deck watching the eagle soar, making ooh and ahh noises. Then it flew to a crow's nest at the top of a cedar tree, swooped down, clutched a crow chick in its talons and flew away. The crow parents were in hysterics.

"Holy shit."

"Oh fuck."

"Man."

"Mother Nature."

"Cruel sometimes or what?"

Silence.

I said, "Let me get some more beer."

Lucy said, "Let me help you."

—

In the kitchen Lucy showed me just how furious she was. "I can't believe Noah revealed that he has cancer at your fucking birthday party."

"You opened the door when you asked why he looked so peaky."

"How was I supposed to know?"

We returned to find the others making idle medical chit-chat.

"Beer for all!" I announced.

"I can't drink at the moment," said Noah.

"Right. Of course." He had been drinking soda all day.

More silence.

"Look," said Tom. "The eagle's coming back."

It was headed right for the same cedar tree. "Oh shit," Tom said.

. . . Swoop.

. . . Shriek!

And off went Mr. Eagle with a second crow chick snack.

Everyone kind of stared at each other. Then Claire's daughter, Simone, eleven, came out on the deck. "Mom, what's double anal? Howard said I should ask you."

My son, Howard, fourteen, was going to get a thrashing tonight, but thank God Simone arrived when she did, because it was very funny, and it broke the mood.

"We'll talk about it in the car headed home, sweetie."

Then Simone saw the eagle. "Mom! Dad! Look! An eagle!"

Yes, our eagle was headed back to the tree.

"Simone," her mother ordered, "get back inside and watch some more TV."

"I want to see the eagle!"

At this point, the youngest three children burst out the kitchen door, wondering what we were all looking at.

"An eagle!" said Simone. "Up there!"

"Cool!"

Lucy then did something she'd once heard would distract people from something bad, which was to drop a large ceramic or glass object onto the floor. She deftly flicked the $300 Spode water jug onto the deck, where it shattered just as baby crow number three was plucked. It didn't work.

"Mom, that eagle just stole a baby chick!" Simone yelled.

The three youngest children shrieked and burst into tears.

"Fuck it," I said, "I'm getting the scotch. Anyone want some?"

All eight adults, Noah included, said yes.

03

Splenda

MY NAME IS OLIVIA. I'm eighteen and I have cystic fibrosis, but I'm okay with it. I grew up in a scary farmhouse in the middle of nowhere. I say scary because my family is superreligious and I'm not—I never was—which has to be genetic or something. My parents believed God would fix my CF, and they only took me to the hospital when I genuinely couldn't breathe. When I was fourteen I had a note prepared and slipped it to the ER nurse. Social services found a lawyer, Adelle, who took on my case pro bono, and she got me out of that scary hillbilly dump.

I'm now into my second life, my real life. I'm realistic that it's not going to be a very long one, and I'm okay with that. I live in a basement suite (*not* the best for CF—mildew) and I have proper medical care, and people come check in on me all the time. I may never again feel as free in my head as I do now. I'm drunk on freedom.

My place is in a neighborhood that's neither urban nor rural. The only time you ever hear about it is when news crews interview local parents who can't believe whatever horrible new thing one of their children has done, things like throwing caribou heads off the freeway overpass. My neighborhood is like that street at the end of *Carrie* where cars drive backwards and bloody hands reach out from the soil to pull you to hell. I just saw *Carrie* for the first time last week. Go easy on me—I'm a pop culture blank. I have five thousand movies and TV shows to catch up on.

I was born on 9/11, which freaked out my parents, who, I think, secretly viewed me as a demon child. On my tenth birthday there was all sorts of 9/11 anniversary buzz, but instead of throwing a birthday party, my parents took me to church in the strip mall beside the auto mall that had just closed down. I remember everyone staring at me like 9/11 was my fault. At the same time, they seemed to be hoping I'd reveal something divine and illuminating. When I turned thirteen, I made the mistake of saying 9/11 was an inside job—I didn't even know what that meant—and a couple of pervy-looking pastors came and interviewed me for four hours. Another reason why I fled.

But I try to forget about all that now. Imagine feeling 100 percent alive every moment of every moment of the day! Maybe that's how animals feel. Or trees, even. I sometimes stare at the plastic bag tree visible from my apartment's ceiling-height window and marvel that both it and I are equally alive and that there's no sliding scale. You're either alive or you're not. Or you're dead or you're not.

A drag queen named Trashe Blanche lives in the other basement suite here. I like her even more than my social worker. She comes over and runs the electric tumbler up and down my back to loosen up the mucus in my lungs. I have to do this sometimes twice a day, because it lessens the chance of airway infections. I've also been taking an antibiotic called azithromycin for years. It makes my burps taste like floor cleaner and I hate it and I want to be Alanis Morissette and get off antibiotics. I want to be part of the world—*your* world.

Yesterday, out of the blue, Trashe gave me a pair of Lana Del Rey knee socks.

She likes to take care of me, I think, just because she's a nice person. Her boy name is Erik, and if Erik doesn't shave for five days, he turns into a handsome overweight guy, but when he turns into Trashe, it makes the whole boy/girl thing confusing, because he/she's equally convincing as both.

Trashe is confused by me, too, always trying to figure out if I'm straight or not. I tell her I'm straight, because I am! But I also tell her that mostly I'm traumatized, because I was raised as a mandatory never-nude. (I just learned that term a month ago.) God, how embarrassing. I always figured I was going to be dead before I ever made it with a guy, so who I'm into was moot. I like it when my doctors are realistic with me, but I know they're lying when it comes to my life span. They tell me I'll live to thirty-five, but because my parents never allowed me treatment when I was younger, I lost probably a decade off my life from all the wear and tear inside my body. I suspect people talk about me the way they do about dogs: "Oh, you know, those large-chested breeds like Bernese Mountain dogs only make it to six if you're lucky. Mutts make it to ten or eleven." I'm one of those short-lived specialty breeds: "You know, those Olivias only go to thirty-five if you're lucky."

Trashe says it would be a shame if I died a virgin, but she doesn't want me throwing myself away on somebody like I'm a skank. "Skank" is another new word in my vocabulary, and I love it . . . skank! It sounds like what it is! The people upstairs from us are a meth-y tattoo artist and his girlfriend, who most definitely is a skank. I truly don't think I'm a skank, but I don't want to die a virgin, either.

Still, the biggest pleasure of my day right now, besides catching up on all the movies I missed growing up, is stealing Splenda packets from fast-food places. Handfuls at a time. I have a drawer full of them and I like to stare at them—I want to have them near me. They're the opposite of the house I grew up in: Scientific. Measured. Clean. And if I mix them with some water and swallow them with my anti-biotics, my burps smell like cheap vodka instead of floor cleaner. When you're me, you take what you can get.

04

Rh_{null}

I MET MY HUSBAND, Steffan, because of my blood type, which is Rh_{null}. You pronounce it "R. H. Null," like it's a Hollywood director from the 1940s. Only about fifty people on earth are Rh_{null}, including me and my thirteen-year-old daughter, Kelli. In order to be born with Rh_{null} blood, two astonishingly rare mutations have to happen at the same time. You're more likely to win $250 million in the Powerball lottery than to have our blood type. If nothing else, when I walk down the street on even the worst day, I can say to myself, Lorraine, your very essence is rare. You're a unicorn.

Of course, that's total BS. Rh_{null} has never done anything for me except complicate my life. Universal donor blood doesn't work on me so, for example, I've always driven wimpy cars so that I won't be tempted to go too fast and crash. And I wasn't allowed to ride a bike: What if I got hurt and needed a blood transfusion?

At eighteen, when I was legally old enough to donate blood, all manner of doctors from around the world turned up on our doorstep. I knew they were coveting my blood for research purposes, but before they asked me for a donation, they always tried to become my friend. Two doctors took me and my parents to swanky hotels for dinner, wooing us with luxury. Two others were so earnest I had to flee. (I never want to hear this line again: "You owe it to humanity.")

Then came Steffan, hot and moustachey and with a French accent. He was from a town called Montpellier in southern France, and he flew all the way just to see me. My parents had gone to Florida for a vacation, leaving me home alone, so it was only the two of us. There was genuine chemistry. I look back at eighteen-and-a-half-year-old me and cringe, but when it was happening, I thought I was queen of the world. Steffan made blood types sexy and fun. OMG, I just reread that previous sentence and I sound like a vampire, but it's true. And after he proposed and I accepted, we drove around the country searching out other blood freaks. My parents were thrilled.

On those trips I got to meet chimeras—people who aren't at all what they appear to be. Like this lumberjack guy named Lars, from Spokane, fully equipped with beard and dick and balls, who was, according to his bloodwork, a woman. And supercentenarians, people older than 110, whose blood Steffan was studying to try to figure out how they got there. I felt like a member of some kind of superclub.

After Steffan and I got married, I moved with him to France, and soon enough I was pregnant. Then Kelli was born with Rh$_{null}$ too, which made me feel way less alone in the world. Life was good. Steffan was part of the international blood-brokering universe and he traveled a lot. Talk about an esoteric business. Depending on where you live, there are all kinds of rules on what you can do with your blood. In some places, selling your blood is likened to selling your body parts and is forbidden. In other places, it's a free-for-all. It's hard to explain, but blood is like diamonds: it's worth nothing and a shit-ton at the same time. I was proud that Steffan kept roaming the globe searching for rare specimens, and I loved the French lifestyle and that my daughter, as soon as she could talk, was fully bilingual.

On Kelli's ninth birthday, it dawned on me that Steffan had somehow changed. It wasn't a big, cosmic revelation. I was icing Kelli's cake and I thought, *Hmmm—Steffan spends more time away than he ever used to.* That's all, but it was definite. That night I tried calling him at the office but couldn't get through, and he missed the birthday cake, which isn't as big a deal in France as it is in the States, but still, come on. He came home late that night and said he forgot because he was zonked after flying back from Cairo. I told him he needed to travel less, and he agreed, but soon enough he was away from home more often than he was with us. Then money seemed to start rolling in, and we bought two new cars and a small, adorable cabin up in the mountains. Was our life suspiciously luxurious for a lab manager with a wife and one child? I'll admit it: I was like Tony Soprano's wife and I wasn't yet ready to ask the tough questions. I also enjoyed our family holidays in Abu Dhabi and Cape Town, and wherever we went, I did as Steffan asked: I donated my blood.

And then came the summer afternoon I was tending my kitchen garden, which, in the south of France, was a marvel to behold. The rosemary alone! I was looking for a chicken manure fertilizer I'd bought a few weeks back and went out to the small barn that served as our garage. I walked directly in on Steffan handing an insulated cooler to a man in return for a wad of euros, like we were in a mafia movie. There was no possible excuse for this.

After Steffan's "client" was gone, we met in the kitchen. Out the window I could see Kelli bouncing on the trampoline with her friends. "Steff," I asked, "I've been donating blood at your request to do my bit for science, but was money the actual reason?"

He took too long to answer. Steffan had evolved into a black marketeer in blood, and there are an astonishing number of very rich and very sick people in the world who will pay almost anything for rare blood types, or for blood from people with specific antigens or mutations that protect them from AIDS or malaria or . . . you name it.

"Steffan, why did you marry me?" I asked.

05

Thong

THERE'S THIS JOKE about 9/11 that you're not supposed to tell because you still can't make jokes about 9/11, but I'm going to tell it anyway.

Knock knock.

Who's there?

9/11.

9/11 who?

You said you'd never forget.

I was asleep with the flu for all of 9/11 and only woke up hours after the attacks were over. I've noticed that a lot of people lie about where they were when 9/11 happened. Unemployed West Coast night owls were all magically awake at 6:45 a.m. on September 11. "And then a friend phoned me to say a plane crashed into the North Tower"—(BTW, why the hell would anyone *do* that?)—"and then *just* as I turned on the TV news, the next plane hit the South Tower!" I've heard this same story from so many people, I wonder if what's really happening here isn't so much a cosmic lie as it is some kind of necessary myth we need to tell ourselves so we feel like one of the gang. Super-FOMO.

You can't figure out who's speaking here yet, can you? Am I male or female? Am I old or young? Am I in a burka? Am I in a wheelchair? Or am I an average guy named Logan who sells Roundup glyphosates and is currently wearing a raspberry-red thong bikini under my jeans because I like the way it makes me feel like a hot teenage girl?

Well, yes, that last one is me. Hi, I'm Logan. I sell poison for a living. As a consequence, I have had to learn how to lie to people: "This stuff is harmless! It's practically a vitamin!"

Here's another universal lie—maybe you've heard it yourself. Ask anyone you know how their trip to Las Vegas went and they will all say, "You know, I don't really gamble much, but before leaving for the airport I played the slots one last time and won [*always*] $150."

I don't know about you, but when I go to Las Vegas, any money I put into a slot machine instantly disappears into a deep, flaming chasm of dead wealth. Yet everyone else makes $150, sometimes even $200, before cabbing to the airport. This one lie is so universal that it makes me wonder if it is encoded in our reptile brain.

But wait—I bet your brain froze back there after you read the words "raspberry-red thong bikini." I can understand that, especially combined with "feel like a hot teenage girl." I think a lot of you now assume I'm gay, but I like to think of myself as a hetero fuck-machine. Surprise!

Women go insane over the thong. Honestly, if you're some poor incel out there, just pop into Forever 21's lingerie department, buy a few thongs, then hit the bars wearing lowrider jeans so gals can see the strap at the top of your butt. Do it, bro!

My older brother's a gay drag queen. No thong for him. He has to duct tape his dick into his butt crack for hours on end while wearing wigs that roast his skull like a toaster oven. And he won't lift anything heavier than a family-sized tin of Beefaroni so he doesn't get "man arm."

Usually, in a family of male children, it's statistically the younger brothers who are gay, but Erik was the eldest of five boys and our only Froot Loop. (He's okay with me saying Froot Loop, BTW.) We even tried to pun on that to create his drag name—Froot de Loop? Not so good. In the end, Erik went with Trashe Blanche.

The rest of us brothers are beanpoles, but Trashe is 125 pounds overweight. She looks like one of those women in horn-rimmed glasses in those old *Far Side* cartoons. She figures she'll spend the rest of her life "circling the continent performing in dive bars and couch surfing, until I die from type 2 diabetes compounded by a sad heart that never even got a chance to be broken."

Trashe wants nothing more than to not be alone, but she created this fierce drag persona that I think scares people away before they get to know her. Me? Forget being with someone else—for now. I'm way too into sex, and I don't "get" monogamy, and I don't get "forever and ever." I see people throwing marriages away because someone slept with a personal assistant or a tennis pro. Why would you do that? You're so morally superior that you can't handle a fling? Grow up. Not everyone wants to be who they're supposed to be 100 percent of the time. Everyone has hidden selves just waiting to pop out. It's who we are.

So, remember what I said about knowing how to lie because I sell poison? There's also a truth I haven't told, which is that twenty-one years ago, I killed a guy. Another thing you weren't expecting, right?

There was blood all over the place—mine and his—but I got away with it. And everything would still be fine if Trashe hadn't let it slip at the Christmas dinner table that she's sent her DNA off to 23andMe. "I want proof positive I was born into royalty and that my current life is one great big swapped-at-birth mix-up."

So I'm waiting for my doorbell to ring one day.

06

Theme Park

HOW DID WE MEET?

To answer that, I have to tell you about my old job. I worked as a mascot at a theme park, and no, it wasn't Disney World. At Disney World they at least put electric fans inside mascot costumes so you don't die of heat stroke in the summer. My park was owned by a Korean consortium on financial life support. No fans for us. I worked there for five years. It was only supposed to be a part-time job to get me through college, but after I learned that the world has no interest in my thoughts on Chaucer, it became full-time.

I'm six foot two, so I played the tall characters, which for me meant alternating between Rooster Rick and Polo the Dog. Please note the cheesiness of the park's mascots.

One thing I liked about being a mascot was that, inside my costume, I could do whatever I wanted and people would think it was just wacky Rooster Rick being wacky and in character. Most of the time it was me trying not to gag from the costume's interior stench of death, given they only got dry-cleaned once a month. The inner lining reminded me of this abandoned red sofa in the lot behind my high school where all the seniors would go every night and fuck their brains out.

I didn't have a handler to ward off the screaming brats who invariably kicked me in the shins to see if I was real. A lot of kids wanted to hug Rooster Rick and pat his belly, which hung right in front of my dick. The park installed a piece of 3/4-inch plywood cap down there. Once a kid punched me there and screamed, "He's hard! Why is Rooster Rick so hard?" LOL.

The parents, of course, were tall enough to catch a glimpse of my face through the black fabric scrim covering Rick's beak or Polo's mouth. People wandering out from the beer garden always did that, and once they saw I was a guy, they left me alone. Hannah, who worked the same shifts as me, occasionally got groped by drunk guys and I had to go to the rescue. Go on YouTube and search "Guy in Lame Rooster Costume Punches Out Drunk Asshole." Over two thousand views as of yesterday. [*Buffs fingernails on pecs.*]

My life changed forever on Fried Chicken Night. A local fast-food franchise, Bell's Chicken, sent their mascot, Miss Belle, to work the crowd. When I saw Miss Belle in the costume area, I was: a) jealous that someone else was competing for my audience, and b) in awe of how nice and clean Belle's chicken costume was. I walked over to her and said, "It must be nice to have a boss who dry-cleans your outfits regularly."

She looked up at me then, and tipped her beak in despair. "Oh, dear God," she said, "I'm a full-time chicken mascot. There's nowhere lower to go."

"I don't know about that. Being a puppeteer might be lower."

"No. When you're a puppeteer, at least there's a chance the audience is thinking, *Hmmm . . . that puppeteer is funneling their subconscious into their characters. This isn't just a puppet show, it's art.*"

"I see what you mean. Inside my costume, I could be bashing my head in total despair at the meaninglessness of it all, and people on the midway would be saying, "Isn't that adorable? That big chicken is New Wave dancing like it's the 1980s!"

A silence fell, and into it I finally said, "I'm Rooster Rick."

With a Southern accent, she replied, "And A'm Miss Belle."

"How long have you been doing this for?"

"Part-time for a year, but as of tonight it's a full-time gig."

"That's pretty much what happened with me. I have a degree in Chaucer Studies!"

"I have one in Sylvia Plath."

Just then my shift manager, Denny, came in, holding an oversized gold novelty key. "You chickens are onstage together in five minutes. Rick, you'll be presenting Belle with this key to the park. After you hand it over, both of you dance. People love it when you costume people dance."

I muttered to Belle, "He can't even bring himself to say the word 'mascot.' Quick: if you could do one thing to leave your mark on the planet, what would it be?"

Belle considered for a moment, then said, "I'd like to create a ring around Earth, like the one around Saturn. Wouldn't that be beautiful?"

"It totally would."

"What about you?"

I thought about it. "I'd like to be a philosopher scientist whose job is to sit alone in a lighthouse for weeks on end trying to think of something else in the universe that could be just as interesting as life, if not more interesting."

Belle came close and looked up at me. Through her scrim, I could just barely make out the face of a person my age. "I like your voice," she said.

"I like your voice too."

From behind us Denny shouted, "You two, onstage! *Scram!*"

From the wings we could see a local AM radio sports-caster at the mike. *Blah, blah, blah . . .* "And now, in celebra-tion of Fried Chicken Night, our beloved mascot Rooster Rick will be presenting the key to the park to the enchanting Bell's Chicken mascot, Miss Belle. Let's have a hand for these two crazy clucks!"

We walked out on the stage, and after I handed Belle the key with a bow, we looked at each other as the music played. It was a perfect moment. Then she tossed the key to the crowd and she jumped my bones right there onstage. Everyone laughed: *Look, Rick and Belle are doing it!*

But we kept right on doing it, and doing it, and after pre-dictable shouts of "Get a room!" people started tossing the bones of their takeout Bell's fried chicken at us.

Finally, Denny chased us off the stage and back to the costume room. Laughing, we yanked off our heads, and then Denny fired me.

"Fine by me," I said.

"Why don't I join you?" Miss Belle said.

Her name turned out to be Sarah. We went out for dinner, where we discovered that we're both vegetarians. Cluck cluck!

07

Airplane Mode

LAST MONTH I HAD TO fly to a drag convention in Florida. I wasn't in full drag on the plane, but my hair was set in a flirty way and I was wearing light makeup, so it wasn't hard to deduce that I was one of those pronoun people everyone talks about. Most of the time, if people comment on the makeup or hair, they'll say something like "You're rocking it, Mama!" and it makes travel fun. But once in awhile you do get a person like the woman in the check-in area for this flight, who wouldn't stop glaring at me, obviously trying to facially convey to me her disapproval of my entire existence.

The thing you learn about being different in whatever way is that maybe half the people you meet would, given full anonymity, open a trapdoor under you that dropped you into a pit of lava. Even the ones who smile at you. *Especially* the smilers. At first, I thought that at least the sour-faced scold in the check-in area was being honest, but then I found out she wasn't content to just scowl.

She ended up one person ahead of me at the security checkpoint, where I noticed the name on her carry-on tag: *Linda Castleberry*. Castleberry? Then I switched my brain into airplane mode, the one you use to tolerate the relentless indignities of air travel. I saw Ms. Castleberry talking to one of the inspectors, who turned to stare at me. *Oh crap, what has this woman done?* I found out two minutes later, when it was my turn to go through the scanner and . . . °Braaap!° I got a fake random.

"If you could come this way with me, sir/ma'am . . ."

The inspector escorted me to a private examination room where two female officers were waiting.

"Please undress down to your undergarments," one of them instructed.

Pat. Pat. Pat.

No problem.

Then the women looked at each other in a you-go-first-no-you-go kind of way until finally the older one said, "Sir/ma'am, do you have anything inside an orifice that we should be aware of?"

That fucking, sour-faced cow Linda. "What? *No!*"

"I'm sorry but we have to check."

"I promise you my mangina does not harbor a minaret-shaped handgun."

But my protests fell on deaf ears and down came the underwear, and inspect they did.

As their rubber-gloved fingers were probing my private places, I devised my revenge.

Once they cleared me, I called my millennial friend and neighbor Olivia and told her what I needed her to do. "But go to the payphone on the corner outside the Circle K to make the call. You need to be untraceable. Please do it now."

"It's cold out."

"Put on ten sweaters."

In the gate area, I walked up to La Castleberry. "I heard the weather is supposed to be wonderful in Florida."

"Did you now?"

"I did." Keeping it light, I mentioned the details of my protracted inspection (which is what she wanted to hear). I got deliberately graphic (which she didn't want to hear).

"When they check your private areas," I said, "they use the tops of their fingers, not the palm sides."

She couldn't help asking me why.

"Because it's scientifically impossible to derive much in the way of erotic stimulus from nerves on the tops of your hands."

"Really?"

"Yes. Also, you in particular might like to know they didn't find a minaret-shaped handgun inside my mangina."

Dagger eyes: "You transvestites pollute the world. You all need medical help."

"I'm not a transvestite. It's called drag, and it's a way of tasting a bit of power you probably never had anywhere else in your life."

The flight was delayed by an hour. Good. More time for Olivia's work to bear fruit. I looked at the clock: *Please, Olivia, don't fuck this up.*

Boarding finally began, and I was behind Ms. Castleberry at the end of the line. When they scanned her boarding pass, it beeped (*YES!!!!!*) and the gate agent's face went blank. She tapped through some windows on her screen and said,

"I'm sorry, Ms. Castleberry, but we can't allow you on this flight. We have credible reason to believe you have a nut allergy, and as a result, you can't board any flight on this airline until the plane has been cleared of peanut fragments."

LOL!

As Ms. Castleberry began to rant, the gate agent signaled to two nearby airport security police, who came and loomed over her. "Ma'am, if you continue to make a scene, these officers will arrest you. It will take twenty-four to forty-eight hours to certify a nut-fragment-free plane to your destination. Go back to the arrivals level and speak with an agent about rescheduling your flight."

As Ms. Castleberry stomped past me, I leaned toward her and whispered: *"For the rest of your life, just before you fall asleep at night, remember this: You are not a good person."*

08

Lube

I'VE NEVER LIKED THE sensation of clothing on my body.
Even something as simple as putting on a T-shirt makes my
skin shudder and I make those involuntary raptor hands, just
like Mr. Burns.

I know that winter climates make this tough, but honestly,
would society disintegrate if we went around naked? So what
if people flash a bit of dick or boob? Are we that horny and
uncontrollable? There's at least some evidence that we're
not: one way to look at the past five hundred years is as a
progression of people wearing successively fewer and smaller
garments. My dad always used to wear a hat and then, in the
middle of 1965, he and every other man in America stopped
and the world didn't end. Maybe in fifty years we'll be walking down the street on Sundays wearing only string ties,
headed off to worship, I don't know, a statue of Walt Disney
made out of depleted uranium.

I got divorced in my late fifties, and after the papers were
signed, I did try going to a few nudist resorts. But something
struck me as not right about women with pancake tits playing
volleyball while their kids sat on the sidelines cheering. It just

wasn't for me. Even though everyone at the resorts would say things like "Golly, we just like the sensation of sun on our skin. Nudist camps aren't about sex," they must not have been walking past the shrubs where Miss Schoolteacher was getting schlonged by the dwarf who leaf-blows the tennis courts.

So, anyway, from that point on, no nude beaches for me, but then one afternoon, there I was on my fenced-in deck—about the size of the kids table at a Thanksgiving dinner—on my condo's roof, responsibly taking in some vitamin D on my recliner, feeling naked and open and free, the way God intended.

At first I was rethinking a spreadsheet I was in the middle of creating at work, but then my mind shifted to Carolina, this foxy little Brazilian number who runs the front desk. Before you know it, okay, sure, whatever, in the privacy of my little deck, I grabbed my tube of lube and started a bit of a hand party.

Eyes shut, I was nearing a conclusion when I heard a whirring noise like a small electric fan. I looked up and there was a drone hovering right above me. *What the fuck?* I jumped up and tried to grab it, but it zoomed out of reach. Then it did a little dance, which let me know that whoever was running this thing was enjoying my situation.

What do you do? Yell? Throw things? Good luck.

I retreated to my condo, where the temperature change was harsh. I breathed deeply for a minute or two, trying to think what to do, then realized I had to go to the cops and report this intrusion on my privacy. But first I made a little iPhone movie of my recliner, and the sightlines onto my fenced deck, to show that I wasn't an exhibitionist or something pervy like that.

I met with Officer Radlett, in his early sixties like me, who asked, "Can you give me a year, make and model of the drone?"

"What? Of course not."

"Welcome to the twenty-first century."

"That's it?"

"What else do you want us to do? If you were underage, I could put out a kiddie porn alert, but you're a grown man."

"I—well, I thought there'd be *something*."

"Nope. Only if someone rewrote the privacy laws, and even then it'd be tough."

"But there's a film of me out there doing you know what."

"Yes, there is." The officer stared at me, smirking maybe just a little bit, and I knew the conversation was over.

Imagine there's a hi-res movie out there of you being intimate with yourself. Wouldn't that change the way you live your day? At any moment, an intern might start to giggle as she walks past you, or the conversation might stop when you enter the lunchroom, or there could be a lone Post-it Note with a drawing of a boner on it stuck on your computer screen when you come back to your desk.

After a few months of waiting for the video to drop, I was sitting at my desk when Troy, our obviously gay office manager, asked if he could see me for a second in the boardroom. As I followed him, I actually wasn't thinking that this would be about the drone footage.

Troy ushered me in, then closed the door behind us. "I'm unsure how to bring this up with you, but I think you ought to see this . . ."

He opened his laptop, and I knew right away.

There was me on my recliner, over the header "Grandpa Polar Bear Punishes His Woolly Mammoth."

I sat down. I mean, what do you think or say?

Troy stopped the stream and closed his laptop. "This was a drone job. I'm guessing. Correct?"

"Yeah."

"For what it's worth, you come across totally hot."

"Thanks."

"Look, 5,802 people have viewed your clip, and it has a 93 percent approval rating. It's kind of a miracle. Nobody likes explicit stuff with guys over forty. Seriously, nobody. Ever."

"This isn't making me feel better."

"Just read the comments. People love you."

Troy flipped up his screen. The first comment: "I'd totally bottom without poppers for this nasty Santa. WOOF!!!"

So now I wear a Speedo on the roof, but I also have a fishing net with a long handle, and I can't wait for my next encounter.

09

Incel

THIS AFTERNOON I SAT beside a drag queen on a flight to Florida and it totally rocked my world. She looked like your ginger-haired high school vice principal dressed like a Monty Python housewife, and every person at the gate wanted to know her story. So, when I sat beside the window and she came and plunked down in the middle seat to my right, I was stoked. I'd also had three vodka sodas in the airport bar and was much less socially awkward than I normally am.

The first thing she said to me was, "Hello, kind sir, could you pass me that safety card tucked in your pocket?"

"Sure."

"I always like to review the exits on any plane I'm flying on. You know, in case we fly into a building or something. What takes you to Miami?"

"My brother's bachelor party."

"Ooh! You better be careful now!"

"I'm not expecting any of the usual stuff from him. He's kind of a wuss. Where are you headed?"

"A drag convention."

"They have drag conventions? Huh. What do you do at them?"

"Mostly we try to figure out ways of recruiting young straight people so we can turn them into flaming homos."

"Oh."

"I'm just fucking with you."

"I figured."

"There are a lot of people who wish we—I—didn't exist."

I thought about this and said, "Me too."

"You? Now why would that be?"

"I'm, uh . . . I'm an incel. You know how people feel about incels."

She laughed. "I can't believe you just said that about yourself."

"It's true. I would definitely like not to be, but I have no choice, because look at me. This is how nature made me."

"You—what's your name?"

"Ben."

"Ben, you could *totally* be fuckable, but only if you change a few things."

I couldn't believe she had the balls to say that to me, even though the thought of actually being fuckable was an answer to a lifelong prayer. "Really? I mean, seriously?"

"Sure. Tell me all about yourself, starting now."

The plane was taxiing. "Well, uh . . . some of the incel clichés are true."

"Like what?"

"Like, I live in a basement and I subsist mostly on energy drinks and junk food."

"Have you ever been laid?"

"I don't know if . . ."

"You've come this far. If you can't tell me, then there's nobody on earth you can tell."

She had a point.

"Once. Three and a half years ago."

She squealed. "You, mister, *you* are going to be my new makeover project."

Truth be told, I've never met anyone as fun to talk to. Somewhere over an American cornfield she asked, "So, my new incel friend, are you a mass shooter just waiting to happen?"

"Of course I'm not. I just find it really, really hard to get laid."

"Your life would be so much easier if you were gay."

"How?"

"Gay guys, at least the ones who live in a city, can get laid almost any time they want."

"Toilet sex?"

Another squeal. "What century do you live in? Sex is more like a handshake with the gays. You get it out of the way and then go on with whatever else it was you were doing before."

"Seriously?"

"Pretty much. Imagine that every time you're horny you can send up a little flare and soon be shagging someone quite plausibly way out of your league—and then two minutes later you're back to regular life. And next time you see that person, there's no drama, no nothing. Or so I've heard. I haven't made it with anyone since the Clinton administration."

"I see the point, but gay sex isn't the answer for me."

"Fair enough. Just wanted to check."

"So, how would you make me appealing to women?"

"How would I do it? I've already been doing it, just talking to you, making sure you're actually a good person and there's not something toxic at your core."

"Did I pass the test?"

"Yes, honey, you passed."

"So, what next? Is it the way I dress?"

She sighed. "How you dress is pretty immaterial to the issue."

"How immaterial?"

"Eighty-five percent."

"How do you figure that?"

"Face is 30 percent. Body is 30 percent. Personality is 25 percent. What you wear? Honest, for a guy? Fifteen percent at most."

"It breaks down that easily?"

"Yup."

"Huh."

"The one catch is that you have to have all 25 percent of the personality or none of the other numbers matter."

As I took this on board, she added, "Don't blame me. Blame the universe."

I didn't have the courage to ask her how she rated my personality; it would have been so much easier if she'd told me that if I just wore a new kind of shirt my sex life would explode.

After we landed, I trailed her to the luggage carousel, feeling boozy and reflective. The scene was suddenly as crowded and noisy as a medieval fish market. A dozen Airbus A380s seemed to have landed at once, and it was all I could do to text her so that she had me in her contacts before entering my brother's bachelor party universe. From across the cartoon-like mob, she shouted, "Don't worry, my little incel. We'll get you laid someday soon!"

I turned red and thought everyone at the carousel would stare at me and judge me a loser, but nobody did, and it dawned on me that most people are totally lost inside their own lives, and that I'd better be getting on with mine really quick, before it was all over.

10

Team Building

CARL TOLD OUR BREAKFAST waitress it was Peg's birthday, and so naturally she brought out pancakes adorned with lit candles. We all sang "Happy Birthday," while around the restaurant people made that "Oh! It's someone's birthday!" semi-smile. At the song's end, Peg blew out the candles to the sound of golf clapping. As you may have guessed, it wasn't actually Peg's birthday.

"Carl, this is so embarrassing!"

"Eat up, birthday girl."

And that was that. Carl is not a funny person and Peg is humorless. The four of us, Carl, Peg, Lance and me, were trapped in Irvine, California, for a four-day conference called Big News on Genetics and Glyphosates. Because of our company's new team building initiative, we had to attend all the seminars and eat all of our meals together.

Team building: does any term more joylessly conjure images of capitalism's Achilles heel? Pretend you like people! Pretend you're having fun! Stay at a hotel that's terrifyingly anonymous! Eat scary hotel food with the same people three times a day when you know all of you would rather be hot-tubbing or napping or getting an erotic massage or even just sitting in your room and staring at a blank wall. (Unless you've tried it, don't knock it.)

At lunch I looked around the restaurant and everyone there was eating, eating, eating, and I felt like I was in a feedlot: 150 chewing jaws; squishy ketchup squeeze bottles making biological sounds. It felt industrial. Lance told me that the main principle driving restaurant dining experiences is plate coverage.

"Plate coverage?"

"Basically, people only perceive value if their plate appears to be fully covered, but it doesn't really matter to them what it's covered with. The single biggest innovation in restaurants in the 1980s was the discovery that one or two melon wedges, properly arranged, can cover up to 25 percent of a plate at a cost of virtually zero."

"How do you know this shit?"

"My dad owns a restaurant."

The waitress emerged from the direction of the kitchen with a slice of cake, and Carl started to sing "Happy Birthday" to Peg again, and we all had to join in. I mean, it would look bad if we didn't. And everyone in the room did the fake smile and, at the song's end, golf clapped.

At breakfast, Peg had been good-naturedly annoyed, but this time she was plain annoyed. Lance and I thought Carl was taking a lame joke too far, but it didn't seem like a big deal.

At dinner, Lance and I both watched Carl to see if he was sneaking over to the hostess to tell her it was Peg's birthday again, but he didn't. The meal was okay, if your definition of fun conversation is pretending songbird populations aren't being decimated (glyphosates!), even though they are.

And then the cake arrived.

Lead balloon.

Peg was totally pissed off. "Carl, why are you doing this?"

"What's the matter? Can't take a joke?"

"Jokes are funny. This is weird."

"Look," said Lance, "the raspberry drizzle covering the plate makes it look like you're getting way more cake than you really are."

At breakfast the next morning, there must have been a rota change, because all the waitstaff were new. At our table, nerves. No eye contact between Carl and Peg, as Lance and I tried to pretend nothing was wrong, just like a family. We had a strained discussion about the day's schedule. The highlight was Lance noticing that they'd misspelled his name on his ID lanyard. Woohoo!

We were almost ready to go when the pancakes with candles came.

Peg was scowling at Carl, but all the other people were clapping and fake smiling, even though they must have been a bit confused because they'd sung "Happy Birthday" to Peg the day before. Anyway, we delivered a cold rendition of the song, after which Peg stormed off.

At lunch, our regional manager, Randy, joined us, so we were on our best behavior. Then the cake came out with sparklers on it. Randy was so excited to sing "Happy Birthday" that Peg had to put a sock in it and smile. Peg and Carl didn't talk to each other for the rest of the afternoon. It was totally Mom and Dad having a fight.

Then came dinner, and Randy joined us again. I had my toes scrunched into shoe fists, wondering what would happen. Randy made a big show of secretly ordering a birthday cake for Peg, and when the cake arrived, I really thought Peg's brains were going to liquify and shoot out her ears, and she made a terrible show of pretending to be grateful while Carl smirked.

Breakfast again. Silence enhanced by hangovers, with strained banter about benzene and phthalate levels in the Missouri River. Peg stared at her plate most of the meal, and Carl tried to be la-dee-dah, as if it were just a normal breakfast.

And then . . . the waitress approached our area with a stack of pancakes with whipped cream, strawberries and sparklers, and Peg totally lost it. She stood up, grabbed the plate and slammed it down in front of Carl, shouting, "What the fuck is wrong with you? I told you to stop! I'm sorry I didn't return the fucking stapler I borrowed from you two weeks ago!"

The restaurant went deadly silent and then some kid a few booths over started to cry. The waitress went over to the child and said, "Don't worry, sweetie, I'll get you another plate of birthday pancakes right away." Another waitress came to our table with dishtowels and spray cleaner and wiped away the mess with a neutral facial expression.

11

Vegan

IT WASN'T LIKE I'D PLANNED a big announcement. It's just that Dad and I had to stop in at the 7-Eleven after the hockey game to pick up whipping cream for Mom. I find the store's signature smell beyond repulsive, like snow tires and hot dog water melting together, but I came inside anyway to witness the remaining shards of the magazine industry dying on the racks. It's so hard to believe magazines were once a thing. Man, Brad and Jen have been almost getting back together for the past fifteen years. Stop it, magazines, just stop it!

I was about to go out to the car when Dad stuck a hot dog (bun/mustard/onions) directly in front of my nostrils.

"Dad, what the—?" And then I puked. It wasn't elegant. I was so embarrassed, I started screaming at Dad, who, to be fair, had only been making a lame dad joke about meat. I remember the confused, smirking customers all staring at me, and the face of a low-wage clerk hating his life.

I'd envisioned, instead, casually mentioning my new dietary regimen while driving with my family through the Sonoma Valley in an electric car that drove like a real car, and not my friend's mom's Prius (which feels like riding in a regular car being towed through sludge). My family and I would see a field of chickens or cows frolicking in the distance, and I would reasonably and calmly mention my opposition to eating anything that came from animals, and we would all discuss my new direction in a civil and pleasant manner.

No such luck. Of course, soon circulating on the internet was a CCTV video of my whole 7-Eleven episode, from three points of view, no less, expertly woven together in real time by those incels from down in the Digital Club, under the header: "Pampered Tween Has Vegan Weiner Meltdown." If there's one thing I've learned, it's that once people see you freak out, they can never unsee you freaking out. It's no fun being the center of a meme, believe you me. At best, people just stare at you. At worst, they make freak-out gestures like the ones I made in the 7-Eleven, accompanied by barfing noises.

My mom told me that I should just hang tight. My meme would soon be replaced by some other meme. (My mother used the word "meme" correctly. Impressive.) After a few days of being humiliated all over the school, I couldn't just stay low and wait for it to pass. I went down to the school basement and confronted the king of the incels, Dylan Hammond. I walked into their lair, saying, "Hello, virgins." Then I went right up to Dylan and said, "Take it down, now."

"Come on," he said. "You gotta learn how to take a joke."

"Not happening," I said, and popped open a can of Pepsi and held it over his laptop keyboard. I told him I would make it my personal life goal to destroy every single piece of technology he owned, so help me God.

He said, "Jeez, don't spaz out. I'm vegan too."

"You are?"

"Yes." And he took the clip down. I know the clip is out in the cloud forever, but the gesture mattered.

That's basically the story of how, two weeks later, we ended up going out on Halloween together. I dressed as a Chicken McNugget and Dylan as a container of honey-mustard dipping sauce. They were really well-made costumes too . . . paper-mache overtop duct-taped cardboard, all painted that unholy McNugget color.

On Halloween afternoon we went to a McDonald's and stood out front trying to pretend we were activists, but most people thought we were part of a McNugget promotion, not a protest. But there was this one woman driving by who saw us and stopped and asked if I was the Freak-out Girl from the 7-Eleven meme, and I was shocked that I felt kind of proud that I was.

Long story short, she was from the local TV news station, and she soon came back with a crew to do an interview, which they afterwards cut together with, ugh, that fucking meme. Dylan and I got to be the color story that night at the end of the local news, just before the weather woman came on. Insert fist bump here.

Is there a moral in here anywhere? Maybe own your notoriety?

I'm still trying to figure that out. I'll discuss it with Dylan tomorrow afternoon while we make hummus and tofurkey for a special Thanksgiving dinner we're throwing just for ourselves.

12

Gum

DEENA'S BUYING A PACK of Juicy Fruit gum, but given the shortage of checkout staff, she has had to spend five minutes waiting in line to buy it. She's buying the gum to get a receipt that establishes where she was at the moment when the guy she hired to break her ex-boyfriend's legs does the deed across town. Video evidence of the purchase will also establish her alibi.

The no-name biker behind her is carrying five massive bags of Styrofoam packing peanuts. He doesn't look like the sort of guy who sells porcelain figurines on eBay that he has to ship to his customers. Still, he seems to be trying to act normal, which is hard to do when, with all of his bags of foam, he looks like one of those people you see in India riding bikes while carrying a thousand empty plastic water jugs. Soon our biker will be getting rid of a body that defaulted on a drug payment, along with the stolen BMW the body is sitting in. He'll empty his Styrofoam peanuts into the vehicle's interior to accelerate his carbecue's speed and temperature.

The next guy in line, Wayne, is waiting to pay for a bottle of lube. He looks a bit squirmy. Decades ago, he read an article saying that super-intelligent people are genetically predisposed to enjoy nudism, and because he perceives himself as intelligent, he's persuaded himself that he dislikes the feel of clothing on his skin. To be fair, he *is* very smart—he's a pattern interpreter for high-end defense contractors. Tomorrow, he'll be nude suntanning on his condo's roof, and it will go all wrong.

Behind him is a woman named Sarah, who has a cling-wrapped tray of a dozen raisin muffins in her basket, among a few other small items. The woman right behind her is Beth, who will see Sarah at a café ten minutes from now. The café will be crowded, so Beth will only be able to find a seat back near the ladies' room, and she'll spot Sarah entering the washroom carrying her dozen muffins. Sarah will stay in there for almost fifteen minutes. When she finally exits, she'll be carrying no muffins. When Beth goes to use the facilities, she will peek into the restroom trash can and find neither muffins nor muffin tray. What happened in there?

Behind Beth is Kellyann, twenty-six, who's buying food for a simple family dinner. Hamburger, cream of mushroom soup, celery, some cookies. Kellyann doesn't realize that earlier this morning she went to work and left her baby in the rear-facing car seat, but she'll soon get back to her car and it will all come back to her.

Then comes Janelle with a home pregnancy test. It will be a boy, IQ of 103, born a week past the due date but with no complications. It is Janelle's first pregnancy, and she and her husband will have a wonderful life with their son. It doesn't get any better than this.

The last person in line is . . . *you?* What are you buying? Do you really need it? Are you buying it because there's something soothing about buying it? Why don't you steal whatever it is you're buying? They'll never notice. Nobody is watching you. Nobody looks at *anyone*, let alone you. Fill your jacket with a dozen bags of Werther's caramels. Who cares! Steal a bunch of discounted *Toy Story 3* plush figures—who gives a fuck? What actually prevents you from stealing this $2.99 crap? Your conscience? God? Habit? What if all of this $2.99 crap was never made in the first place? That might actually be a better world to be living in.

What's this? Deena, our gum shopper, has just received her receipt for a twenty-stick pack of Juicy Fruit. Next in line, please.

13

Unleaded

WHY ARE SOME PEOPLE alcoholics? It's because Mother Nature wants the seeds of fermenting fruits to be eaten and then scattered as widely as possible. We're talking about 100 million years of evolution here. Birds do it. People sure as hell do it.

Simple explanations are best. Take it from me, as someone who once fucked around almost all the time: if you want to keep getting laid while keeping your spouse in the dark, don't mess around with that woman from the Nordstrom's perfume counter or the millennial gym trainer hooked on Old Spice. If you ever get hit with a surprise perfume bomb from someone you hook up with online, stop at the gas station on the way home and sprinkle some unleaded 87 on your hands. You can say you spilled it while filling up, but you can't use that excuse too often.

Harder to conceal is lipstick on your briefs. Don't risk the home laundry basket. Throw them out before you come home. If your spouse notices, confess that you sharted after a sushi working lunch with the software development team. Let laughter be your cloak.

I was incredibly unfaithful to my wife. I slept around while she was dying; the worse she got, the more I needed the sex. During the six weeks Leah was in palliative, I probably laid someone new at least once a day, as well as once by a repeater.

I'm good-looking, and I know it. I'm among the 5 percent who generate 95 percent of online hookup traffic. Our species needs reasonably good-looking guys like me to keep the species going or else we'll all start looking like goitered hill-billies with pretzel teeth. The Queen of England breeds horses; nature has bred me to create hotter humans. I sound like a dick. I am a dick. That's what I'm trying to tell you here. Leah was at the end of stage 4 pancreatic cancer and I was out behind the KFC, dumpster-fucking its day manager, Sheera. I walked away from that encounter with the memory of Sheera's wicked smile and a twelve-piece barrel plus cole-slaw, which I brought to the hospice, knowing that Leah could only eat Jell-O. Still, she said it reminded her of how much she missed real food, and we had a small cry.

Dick.

Leah's relatives treated me with such understanding that when I said I needed some time to myself, they gave me those wet, commiserating beagle eyes. Instead of being home in the den, weeping over albums filled with photos of Leah, I was in a twenty-second-floor waterfront apartment doing a three-way with two young women in third-year engineering, Gina and Andrea. It was the first time I had ever let something, anything, be put up my butt, and I have to tell you, the experience opened a lot of doors for me. Don't judge what you haven't tried.

I guess it's just that I had a life—Leah and I had a life—that we'd built over the years: young, successful and loving couple about to have kids . . . and then cancer. But even before the cancer, I knew that I was not meant to be Mr. Successful Guy with a Wife. I was at the age when it had just dawned on me that this life was the only one I was going to get. Man, did that chill me. So what does a guy who looks like me do? I started sleeping around.

When it got close to the end, I started reading the obituaries. I'd never done that before, but I needed to see how obituaries are written—how long they usually are and what they're supposed to say. Most of them ran with a photo, sometimes of an old person when they were young, or of a sick person when they were well. I figured that was what I would do for Leah. I even checked out the cost so I'd be prepared, and found out that because obituaries are one of the few remaining items newspapers make money on, they charge an insane amount of money.

Once I got started, though, I got sucked into the archives, going back years and years. Every so often I'd see one for the mom or dad of a high school friend, or a random acquaintance from earlier in my life. Every time I dipped in, it would take me a little while to realize that I'd already seen some of the obits. Face it, a lot of old people look very similar, especially old white guys. Usually it would take something like a weird haircut or an emotional opening line to remind me that I'd already read about the person.

And then came the day when Leah, who I truly did love, chose to say goodbye. My state doesn't have Death with

Dignity laws, so Matteo, her palliative care worker, said I needed an alibi for where I was at the time of Leah's departure. He told me to drive across town and buy something small in a store that has a lot of surveillance cameras, to establish date and time. I picked up the weirdest feeling from him, like he was happy I wouldn't be there when he helped Leah die. Anyway, so there I was across town in some store's lineup, looking on my phone at the faces of potential online hookups, many of whom I'd swiped past hundreds of times already. And then it hit me that scanning their faces was like scrolling through the online obituaries every morning and trying to remember if I'd already seen a dead person's photo.

What makes a person memorable? Beauty? Age? Good lighting? A winning smile? A bad sweater? Ugliness?

Too late. The moment I made that connection, my libido died. I haven't had sex since.

14

Lego

ONE DAY THE PRINCIPAL called me and my best friend, Dylan, into his office. "The school fair is coming up and I want the two of you involved in it," he said. "You only have four months to go before we release you out into the universe and, down the road, I want you to at least have one fun memory of this place."

Dylan said the school fair sounded kind of hokey and I hemmed and hawed.

"Humor me," the principal said.

He was basically guilting us into doing something we really didn't want to do, but it was nice that he at least treated us like grown-ups, and so we caved.

"What do you want us to do?" I asked.

He reached into his desk drawer and removed a huge pile of Starbucks cards. "I can see your eyes lighting up. You vegan kids always love coffee."

We certainly do, and we were talking five-dollar cards here. Maybe this wouldn't be so bad.

"Okay, so the deal with Starbucks is that we give the cards

away as people come into the fair, but each person has to do something before you give them a card."

"Like what?"

"I don't care. Ask them a skill-testing question. Just make sure no one dies and nothing sexual happens. I want you here at the school at five p.m. tomorrow, when the fair starts. And I forgot to say, you can keep a few of the cards for yourself."

I admit that Dylan and I left the office a bit drunk with the power of having all of that loot to divvy out. I guess this is how corruption starts, though we actually gave it our all trying to think of something truly cool people could do to get their card. We tossed ideas around all the way to the mall, where Dylan wanted to use a new stop-frame app on his phone to photograph people moving around like ants, which is kind of cliché, but the app really did make the end product look more professional.

Just as we were wrapping up, this kid, maybe nine, came out of a toy store screaming at his mother like an overindulged junior asshole in the making. He grabbed the bag his mom was holding and yelled, "This is the worst present ever! I can't believe you did this to me!"

The world's worst present turned out to be a huge box of off-brand Lego-like plastic bricks. The kid hucked the box onto the floor and ran off. His mother looked at the box, then at us, shrugged and went off to deal with the rest of her life.

Dylan picked up the fake Lego box and said, "I have an idea."

After school the next day, we used red duct tape to tape off a rectangle maybe twelve steps long on the concrete outside the front door, and filled it with the plastic blocks. Then we made a big sign that read THE LEGO WALK OF FIRE! TAKE THE DARE AND WIN BIG! The deal was that you had to take your shoes off and walk the walk, and at the end you got the five-dollar Starbucks card. Just before the fair started, the principal came by to tell us we were rock stars and he knew we'd go far in life if we kept trying this hard.

People loved it, and we were handing out cards like mad, so we decided to make it harder. I made the genius observation (thank you) that it would be a lot more painful to do the Lego Walk of Fire if there were *fewer* bricks, so we paused operations to remove a strategic two-thirds of them. So much pain! As people did the walk, wincing in their sock feet, we'd shout encouraging things like "Pretend it's three in the morning and you are so sleepy you can't keep your eyes open, but you have to go pee." People seem to like pain. Lots of them did it a few times, even though we could only give them one card.

Then this guy showed up who looked a little bit like he lived in his car—or maybe worse. He said he'd graduated from the school in 2013 and wanted to see what it looked like these days. He stood for awhile watching people do the walk of fire and was pretty mellow, but then he started doing this weird tuneless whistling.

Why do people whistle tunelessly? It makes you look so guilty and up to no good. Of course, when he started up with that, Dylan had to be a smartass and said, "Sounds to me like someone here got molested by their football coach." The guy's sunburned face turned white. He stopped whistling, stared at us for a long moment, then walked away. Soon after, we ran out of Starbucks cards, picked up our blocks, balled up the duct tape and shut down our special event.

Cut to three hours later. Dylan and I were at my place, watching *Princess Mononoke* in frame-by-frame mode, when the doorbell rang. Mom answered it and then she called us down and there were a couple of cops in the doorway who wanted to know what we'd said to the homeless guy.

I said, "Wait. What's going on here?"

It turns out that, after he walked away from us, Mr. Class of 2013 headed to a nearby suburb, where he climbed over the fence and into the backyard of the house where his old high school coach lived. He grabbed some tiki torches from by the pool and ran inside and attacked him, yelling that at last someone had believed him, that the two kids running the walk of fire at the school knew the truth. The coach, a big guy, was strong enough to fight him off, and didn't suffer even a scratch. The drifter guy got a huge gash in his leg and ran off leaking blood.

"What do you know that can help us? Anything that might help us find him?" asked one of the cops.

I thought about it. "Maybe Starbucks?"

15

Resting Bitch Face

DO WE BECOME OUR FACE, or does our face eventually reflect who we are? I've never thought of myself as being unattractive, but ever since kindergarten I've noticed that people tend to be wary and suspicious when they need to deal with me. It's as if they expect something to go wrong. There's maybe a hint of dread in there too. When I went out trick-or-treating with the other kids, everyone else got a smile with their treat, but I got a blank face. And even now everybody expects me to be the mean girl. At what point did I take on this role? Which came first, the bitch or the face? I am not the mean girl.

Recently I went to my dentist, Vaughn, who, after installing a crown (I had tried to eat a toffee apple at a Halloween party), pulled up a chair. "Kim," he asked, "how do you feel about your smile?"

"My smile? Great, I guess." We'd just finished an astonishingly expensive two-year journey of invisible braces and near-total dental reconstruction. "It's been a long haul, but it's been worth it."

"Right. Good."

"Vaughn, there's something you're not saying, isn't there? Please tell me no more braces—I don't think I could take more braces."

A small laugh. "Braces? No. You're great that way."

"Great *that way*? In what ways am I not great?"

"Well . . ."

"Well?"

"If I gave you a piece of advice, would you consider it?"

"Advice? From you? Of course."

"It's nothing major. Please, don't worry. It's just that . . ."

"Just what?"

"Some of my patients have had excellent results using targeted muscle deactivation."

"Wait—you mean Botox?"

"Yes."

To be honest, it felt kind of glamorous to be discussing Botox, like my life had been upgraded, but why? "I have my mother's Irish skin," I said. "I don't think there are that many wrinkles to tweak."

"Well, it's not so much wrinkles."

[Awkward silence]

"Vaughn, you're not telling me something. What are you not telling me?"

"Kim, relax. I just think that if a few select locations on your face were properly targeted, it could alter your overall . . . aura considerably."

"Vaughn, stop pussy-footing around!"

"Okay, okay. It's just that you have RBF—resting bitch face—and you could fix that."

Time froze. The room surrounding me became a painting: I saw myself semi-reclined on a reclining vinyl seat the color of all human skin tones averaged out; MSNBC on a screen up near the ceiling on mute, with its endless numerical monetary crawl on the bottom; the sound and smell of someone else's molars being drilled one station over from mine. It was the medical equivalent of an airport bar.

Finally I got it out. "You think I look like a bitch?"

"We both know that's not what I'm saying."

"But it is. Why else would you call it resting bitch face?"

"Because that's what it is."

"You say that like you're describing freckles or eye color."

"We've only been able to isolate it as a medical condition recently."

"It's a medical condition?"

"Bad term on my part. I meant a condition in general. Something that, once pointed out, can never again be unnoticed, but that can also be rectified."

"Is ugliness a condition too?"

Vaughn was getting exasperated. Frankly, good for me for putting him in that position. "Kim, I really didn't want you to take it as an insult, because it's not."

"Just that I'm a bitch, is all."

"It's just that when you let your face slip into neutral, you do look a bit aggressive. I mean, Kim, this is stuff they discuss on *Ellen* and *Oprah*. That stupid TV is on for half of my waking life. I know you've heard of resting bitch face before. Don't shoot the messenger."

"Okay, okay." And I remembered all the guys I liked who

never asked me to dance, and every time I heard girls call me "Clenchy" behind my back: *You know, you could stick a pencil between Kim's butt cheeks and it'd stay there all day.*

And then I had to recognize the kindness of my dentist for naming the beast—and offering a way to kill it. The glamor of Botox.

I asked, "So, which muscles would you temporarily deactivate in order to make me not look like a bitch?"

"It's kind of amazing what we can do these days. Let me show you some case studies." And voilà, as if from nowhere, he produced an album filled with RBF before and after shots.

Honestly, if the glass-block walls had pulled back to reveal a studio audience, I would not have been surprised. Who doesn't love a good makeover?

"Ooh, look at her. In that first shot she looks like she'd key your car if she thought you took her parking spot. And here she looks like she bakes cookies for the poor sick kids you see on telethons."

"Amazing, right?"

"And her! She went from mug shot to red carpet."

"Ta-da! I do think some injections would change your life, Kim."

"I'd look more approachable, basically."

"Yes, and, you know, uh, I think I might even ask you out."

"Wait. You're asking me out?"

"Well, sort of."

"But only if I get Botox?"

"It's not that cut-and-dried."

"You're an asshole."

16

Lurking Account

IF A WOMAN EVER PAUSES in the middle of her day and asks herself, *Hmmm . . . I wonder if my husband is having an affair*, then the answer is yes. There are a trillion signals that may have made you wonder—nature built you that way— but yes, he is. When you ask that question, you already know the answer.

This is all to say that I've got cancer and I don't have much longer to live. My husband's been fucking around like crazy since this all began. He thinks I don't know, but I do, and I actually don't mind—not because I'm a saint, but because I'm in love with Matteo, a nurse here at the hospice.

When Duncan shows up, he does put on a good grieving show, but it's total horseshit. My mom thinks he's a saint, but she doesn't have any of those unholy hook-up apps on her phone. Matteo and I have fun going through my phone in lurk mode to see how Duncan's pimping himself that day: *I love nature and long hikes. I'd like nothing more than to hand-stain a premium cedar shingle roof over the course of a week, with a cooler full of Bud and a friendly lady with me to watch the stain dry while the sun sets.*

Oh, Duncan, you are embarrassing.

Matteo gets in bed with me the moment the coast is clear. You're maybe thinking, *Yuck! Making it with a scrawny cancer lady!* But you're wrong. I have a non-wasting cancer, like the cancer that actors on TV shows get when their character has to die but they still need to look good. Matteo is fucking hot. I can say that—I can say anything since I'll be dead in two weeks—but yeah, Matteo is insanely hot.

When Duncan comes in and does his brave husband routine, I lie there trying not to laugh. He'll have spent the day bonking desperate women and then he brings me a teddy bear and my mother thinks he's God. In some weird way, I guess, he and I are both getting exactly what we want, and our mutual duplicity makes our actions feel less like betrayal to me. Duncan's not a bad guy. He's handsome enough, and, I mean, I *did* marry him. But he's not an old soul.

Matteo *is* an old soul who also happens to have a beer-can dick. I'm about to die and I'm having the best sex of my life. How does that make sense? But it does. People look at me lying here smiling and think, *She's so brave.* I'm actually not brave. Death scares the shit out of me like it scares most people, except the universe handed me Matteo to see me through. I'd love to die while we are making it, but I know that won't happen. I'm the first death in my family, so they are all going to be standing around looking grim and wondering what my last moment will look like. Maybe they expect to see a cartoon ghost float out of my chest. No, that's too old-fashioned. Maybe I'll reboot like a video game. I don't care. I'll be gone.

My decision right now is whether to tell Duncan that I know he's been sleeping around, and that I have too. He could have been *slightly* more respectful, given my situation, but who am I to judge? While Matteo was giving me a foot massage this morning, the nurses who passed by all smiled. They think Matteo's gay.

Is there anything to be gained by letting Duncan know? Not really. Will it change who he is as a human being? Definitely not. All those nights he came home with his hands smelling like gasoline—I read in *Cosmopolitan* ages ago that it's a cheater's number one way of concealing incriminating odors. Or maybe it was online somewhere. Google it.

The one thing that genuinely surprises me in all of this is that I did need to tell *someone* about Matteo. If I didn't, I thought I'd explode. But who? Someone in my family? Noooooo way. My lawyer? Yawn. Girlfriends? They wouldn't understand. Weirdly, I ended up calling this guy I worked with at the Gap a million years ago. Erik is the only non-judgmental human being I've ever known. I'd lost track of him, but a mutual acquaintance gave me his number, and he actually phoned me back when I texted him. When we said hello, it was as if no time had passed. He was at the hospice within an hour.

He's gay, and old enough that he lost lots of friends to AIDS. When he arrived, he knew all of the older staffers, who greeted him like Marilyn Monroe about to perform for the troops in Korea.

"Sweetie," he said, when he showed up at my door, "you look radiant for someone being written out of the soap opera."

We held hands and our eyes began to leak. I told him everything, beer-can dick and all, and nothing surprised him. When Matteo showed up after shift change, Erik greeted him like an old friend, and we all threw our arms around each other.

"Leah, did you enjoy life on earth?" Erik asked after the hug was over.

"What a weird question. But yeah. I did."

"Matteo, do you love Leah?"

"I do."

"Leah, do you love Matteo?"

"I do."

"Well, in that case, in your own special way, you two crazy kids are now married."

Erik discreetly left the room, and I looked at Matteo and realized that, yes, we were.

17

Hip Hotels

I'M SUE. I work for the world's most chic hotel chain. My job is to travel undercover to each of their many fine hotels and secretly note absolutely everything I see there that's done incorrectly. Did the concierge wait for more than one ring to pick up the phone? Was that the correct fork with the sole? *Everything.* And you have no idea how fussy I can be. I may look like your younger sister's best friend, but I can also be a total dick if you give me any lip—but a stealthy dick. Three weeks after my visit, you'll be wondering why you've been demoted to valet parking manager, never suspecting that it was because of the "guest" who was so unhappy with your service.

You don't get much sympathy when you have a job like mine. *Oh . . . woe is me! I'm getting calluses from trying on too many plush white bathrobes. These complimentary sleep masks are chafing the bridge of my nose and have the faint odor of off-gassing plastic. Were they made in China?*

I basically landed in gravy. Sometimes I think of people whose undercover jobs aren't quite so cushy as mine, like those air marshals who sit incognito on roughly half of all civil aviation flights in the US, especially now. Think about that for a second: imagine having to be a passenger on United Airlines every working day.

Given my job, I totally identify with that crazy Korean woman who forced a KAL flight attendant to get down on her knees and grovel for mercy for giving her a bag of peanuts instead of a ceramic dish filled with mixed nuts heated to 63 degrees Celsius. "Nut Rage" they called it on CNN. Good. I get nut rage all the time, though I would never lash out so obviously at undertrained morons. It's why I'm always extra-hard on rating hotel gyms; if I don't burn off steam, I'll turn into one big massive stress cold sore. By the way, next time you see that a hotel gym is under renovation, it means they just don't want to pay to insure the gym. Gyms are lawsuit magnets, like motel diving boards in the 1960s.

My life is actually pretty lonely. I have to be away from home for weeks at a time, and the country and the season can make it worse, like Germany in winter. However, I have a plan: I'm going to snag a rich guy. Okay, so not the most feminist of goals, but I don't want to be fifty and still running around ensuring that Keurig coffee labels are arranged with their logos baseline-flush in a neat line in some air-conditioned crypt in Singapore.

If you're a guest at one of my chain's hotels, you've got access to dough, but how much of it is really yours and not the company's? I find that the big spenders are usually on an expense account. The moment they have to actually pay for something themselves—you can't charge the silk scarf in the hotel gift shop to your room, for instance—their faces crumble. You might even notice a Costco membership card peeking out from behind the Amex Black.

Fact: genuinely rich guys wear linen, and the more wrinkled it is, the bigger their ski chalet. They also avoid wearing socks whenever possible. Someone once told me smart people like being nudists; I'm telling you rich people hate socks. And mostly, genuinely rich guys try to stay under the radar. See that guy over in the corner of the dining room sending back a bottle of Moët something because it displeases him? He probably makes one-point-three a year for a pharmaceutical company, but he's low on assets and likely has an ex. See that guy drinking a Diet Coke and reading *The Economist* on an iPad? *Zoing!*

That guy's name is Orazio, which is Italian for Horace, so you'd think he's Euromoney, but he's actually from central California, where they grow broccoli and olives and marshmallows or whatever else comes from there. He's two years older than me and single but not gay. I know all these things because I tipped the desk clerk a bottle of white wine to tell me his name (forget cash: hotel staff love treats) and then visited LinkedIn—the SkyWest Airlines of websites—and I got the job done.

So how did Horace get rich? By patenting a shit-ton of GMO- and Roundup-friendly agricultural products. His high school buddies on LinkedIn all send him fist bumps and high fives, but guaranteed, their souls are corroding as though basting in battery acid.

I just noticed that the waiter didn't put a coaster beneath Horace's Diet Coke. That's a demerit point. Two, actually, because it was a flat-out clueless error.

Q: Why is a very rich man like Horace having a Diet Coke by himself at 4:45 in the afternoon?

A: Because he's rich enough that he can.

"I'm only a guest here," I say to Horace, "but let me give you a coaster."

"What? Oh—that's okay."

"No, it's not. They also gave you a slice, not a wedge, of lime. That's not right."

"I love limes. I actually grow them."

"You must live somewhere sunny. Let me guess . . . Fresno?"

"Wha—!!! How did you . . . ?"

"Wait—seriously? You're from Fresno? OMG, I just pulled that out of a hat. I always thought Fresno was where they grew marshmallows and Halloween candy."

He chuckles. "I wish it was that interesting. Sit down. Can I buy you a drink?"

"Well . . . okay. Why not."

"What's your name?"

"I'm Sue."

"Hello, Sue. My friends call me Orazio."

18

23andMe

IN THE EARLY 1980S a gang from college, eight of us, would have our annual party weekend at a cabin owned by the family of my friend Dean. The year we had what turned out to be our final party, none of us were yet married, but we'd stopped being YOLO and were at that point in our lives when we'd started believing in all that find-yourself BS.

Dean had gotten fired from his job because he was smoking too much weed—this was back when weed meant prison time. He might have been okay except he'd gotten paranoid at work one time too many, something along the lines of "Who ate my celery sticks? Someone in this office ate my celery sticks and nobody leaves until someone owns up to it." Anyway, Dean's dark side was emerging, and our annual weekends had grown more creepy than fun. Once he had us in his power up there, it was either Dean's way or the highway. For example, we'd always played drinking games, and Dean had always been in charge of them, but his punishments became bizarre. If you couldn't down a yard-long beer, you'd have to eat/drink a gas station sandwich that had been run through a blender and fortified with two shots of tequila. If you refused to do that, he'd say stuff about your sister that was . . . disturbing.

This was long before the internet and smartphones, but if we had owned smartphones, on the way home we would have all been texting each other: *I don't think I'll be going to Dean's again next year.* We were too old for lost weekends.

So Dean dropped away from us.

The following summer I ran into Dean's brother at a bar, and he told me Dean was now living alone in the cabin and that none of the family really saw him. I was too wrapped up in my own life to take this on board, and soon forgot about it.

The next December Dean phoned me to ask what weekend in January we wanted to come up. I was caught off guard and fumbled my way through a pathetic mass excuse for the whole bunch of us. I could imagine Dean's irises doing that reptilian flare they did as I spoke. I felt so guilty that when I was getting off the phone, I offered to drive up for an overnight visit on my own the next weekend. His response was a hmmm. Uh-oh.

The visit was a disaster. The house stank of ganja. The moment I showed up, Dean laid into me about what phonies we all were, especially me. "I've never trusted you," he said. "And it looks like I was right." He was dressed like he was living out of a car, not in the cabin, and he smelled like it too.

Then I got mad myself. I didn't need this shit. I ended up running out to my car and tearing away, with him chasing me down his lane and onto the gravel road, shouting "Phony!" and throwing stones at my car.

Come the next June, I had a new girlfriend, Casey, who wanted to be a therapist. I told her about all my friends, including Dean. She listened closely, then looked at me with big, sincere eyes and asked, didn't I think Dean needed a true friend, someone who'd take the bad with the good? Yeah, sure, whatever.

In September, Casey went away for a week to her cousin's bachelorette at the same time I had scheduled a week's holiday, and suddenly I had time on my hands. One night around sundown, I was drinking some beers alone, and I got sentimental and thought, *You know what? Casey's probably right. Dean just needs a friend. I'm going to go see him right now.*

I arrived in the dead of night. The streets of the cottage town were deserted. This was long before mountain biking and winter sports stuff: when Labor Day came, the place shut down.

As I drove to the cabin along the unlit gravel road, I was unsure if this was such a hot idea. Listen to me—now it sounds like I'm telling a horror story, which I am.

At Dean's cabin, one outside light was on, surrounded by a halo of insects. The front door was open by maybe a hand's width. I called through the crack, "Dean? Are you there, man?" and poked my head in. The stench made me gag and pull the door shut.

I took a deep breath of fresh air, plugged my nose, opened the door with my elbow and flipped on the light. The place looked like a homeless encampment and smelled like rotting flesh. I assumed Dean had died, and went into Boy Scout mode, turning on the lights as I walked through the place, so familiar from our old parties, looking for the worst.

The worst turned out to be the cabin's bulk freezer, which was filled with hundreds of frozen meals made by Dean's mother and for some reason was now unplugged. When I lifted the lid, the tubs and bags were filled with maggots. How do they even get into something covered in plastic?

Gagging, I turned around and there was Dean, so close to my face I could feel his breath.

"Ah. So the phony returns," he said, and stabbed me in the armpit with a hunting knife.

"What the fuck!" I yelled, and pushed him off me. His head hit the corner of the kitchen counter and he went down like a dead fish, twitched a bit and died. It had been sixty seconds since I'd opened the cabin door.

I ripped off my sweatshirt and stuck it in my armpit to stop the bleeding. I staggered around wiping down everything I'd touched, and decided there was nothing I could do about the blood. At least nobody knew I'd been here, and I'd left no fingerprints. I turned out all the cabin lights, got into my car and drove away.

This was before security cams. This was before *CSI*. I couldn't have killed Dean more easily if I'd planned it. I got away with it and lived more than twenty-one years with the crime still unsolved, at which point my brother announced he'd sent a sample of his saliva to 23andMe.

19

Sharpies

THE GUY WAS SITTING on the sidewalk outside the liquor store, panhandling. He was maybe a bit younger than me, holding a cardboard sign that said EVERY LITTLE BIT HELPS and, below that, HAVE AN AWESOME DAY. When I walked past him, he said, in sarcastic mumble voice, "Yeah, you have a good day too. Have a real good day." I glanced back at him and noticed he had a big gash above his knee. If his entire tableau could speak, it would say one word: "drugs."

It's not like I'm some big angel in the drug department, so who am I to judge? I went into the store and looked around for a bottle of a chilled unoaked white with a screw top, not a cork, but not because cork trees are becoming endangered with global warming and all. I just wanted to be able to open the bottle on the bus. Oh, did I mention it was raining? It was, and it was dark, too—that darkness you get every fall when the days grow shorter.

The liquor store was lit like a surgery theater, which flattered none of the customers' complexions. *Dear Liquor Store Owner: Why on earth would you light your store so brightly? We all come out of it looking bad.* At the till, a woman my age in a raincoat was rummaging through an almost comically oversized black cloth purse for money.

The guy at the till asked her if she minded if he rang through other customers until she found the money. (She was buying a twelve-ounce bottle of rum. Hard-core.) She nodded. I stepped ahead of her and paid for my discount bottle of Pinot Grigio and went back out on the street. The rain had stopped and the world felt calmer, like when they lower the music volume in a noisy restaurant. I went over to the Sneery McSneerface panhandler and crouched down to speak with him.

"What do *you* want?" he hissed.

I said, "Two things. First, what's your name?"

After some hesitation he said, "Isaac. What's the second thing?"

I said, "Isaac, I want to give you twenty dollars."

Isaac looked at me like I was trying to lure him into a hobo fight in the back alley. "Why do you want to give me twenty dollars? What's your game?"

I said, "No game, Isaac. Consider the twenty bucks a kind of investment in your business."

He said, "This is freaking me out. And why did you ask me my name? That's just weird."

"I asked you your name because people can reach a point in life where days can go by and nobody ever calls them by their name."

Isaac went quiet.

"Right," I said. "Let's discuss your location here, Isaac. You're on the curb outside the entrance. Why on earth would you set up shop here? Move that way twenty feet and you're right by the exit. People leave the store in a better mood than when they went in, and they usually have change."

Isaac said, "That's actually a good idea. Thank you."

"Next, let's look at your cardboard sign."

I picked it up and we looked at it like he was a student in a drawing class.

"You've used two different colored Sharpies on this sign. The top part is sans serif, and the bottom is a serif. Not only that, but you felt-penned the edges with the blue."

Isaac said, "It makes it look a bit nicer."

I said, "Yes, it does. Well done. And finally, let's discuss your overall attitude, Isaac."

"My attitude?"

"Yes, your attitude. I heard your snotty comment as I walked into the store, and here's the thing: if you're smart enough to use middle-class guilt as a marketing tool and to invent two new fonts from scratch and make a great-looking sign, then you're basically too smart to be out here doing this."

Isaac said, "I know, but it's just not that easy."

From behind me, a woman spoke, startling both Isaac and me. "Ask me my name. Please. Ask me."

Huh? I turned and there was Rumwoman.

"Sure," I said. "What's your name?"

"Julie."

Together Isaac and I said, "Hi, Julie," and she started to cry.

Isaac gestured for her to join him on his cardboard floor, and she sat down, still crying.

Isaac said, "Don't cry, Julie. Things will be okay."

"Did you hear all of what we were saying?" I asked.

She said, "Yes, I did. I couldn't find any money in my bag, and I came out of the store right after you."

I sat down too, and asked Julie if she'd like a sip of Pinot Grigio.

"Please," she said, wiping her cheeks.

So I unscrewed the wine bottle and handed it to her.

After scanning for cops, she took a swig. "Man, when you're in my universe, this shit's like Kool-Aid," she said, and offered the bottle to Isaac, who waved it away.

"No thanks. I don't drink."

We shared a quiet moment, and then Julie said, "So, what happens next?"

I said, "What happens next is the three of us walk to Emergency and get the gash in Isaac's leg fixed."

20

Romcom

I REALLY DON'T KNOW why I'm alive. I mean that in a general sense that has nothing to do with self-pity or fishing for sympathy. I'm just being practical. I'm past child-bearing age. I have little family and no friends, just a few acquaintances. I work a disposable job at a chain restaurant. I contribute zilch to society. I could evaporate tomorrow and not a ripple would pass through the world. I have a bit of money saved for retirement, but retirement from what? Nothingness?

I guess my aging body will eventually generate more revenue for hospitals and the medical system. It's the dirty little truth about the system: healthy people are bad for capitalism. Fat, sick, broken people are the engine of our economy.

I find it ironic that, in spite of my generalized uselessness, if you killed me, you'd still be sent to jail for murder. I sometimes wonder if serial killers are disappointed with themselves when they kill a nobody like me. All the notoriety they'd gain from me would be as a tidbit for a boring podcast a few years down the road. They wouldn't even name me. They'd just say, "Victim Number Three was a fifty-two-year-old single woman," and leave it at that.

I used to date, but I never found The One. I'm not even sure how many The Ones there are out there, but by the time I figured out there was never going to be a The One for me, I was set in my ways and the thought of making do with someone merely passable was intolerable. Sure, I've watched my share of romcoms where the heroine ends up with someone implausibly out of her league, and there's a part of me that still thinks, *Maybe one day* . . . But then my realistic inner voice reminds me that at my age The One would probably drain my bank account and give me syphilis.

In spite of everything I've just said, I find myself not wanting to be dead. Talk about the most awkwardly couched expression of the will to live ever uttered, but no, I still choose being alive over being dead.

It may be my skewed point of view, but I think there are a lot more people like me out there than there were even a decade ago. The electronic universe allows us to travel so deeply inward, hardly anyone ever looks up from their phone to make sexy eyes with a stranger on the subway.

I often think about what it means to have a personality. Hailey is a scatterbrain. Sebastian is super-serious. Anne is a Debbie Downer. Neil is the life of the party. Carrie is always oversharing. Ben won't make eye contact. They all have traits, but are these traits perhaps medical in nature? Is the unwillingness to make eye contact a sign of being on the spectrum? Is oversharing a sign of thwarted sexual impulses? Does Debbie Downer need amphetamines? At what point does personality end and psychopathology begin?

Some years ago, I bumped into Adrian, a bank teller I used to work with. When I knew him, Adrian was a very buttoned-down kind of guy, but when I saw him midsummer on a street corner, he was wearing black-leather almost bondage-y gear. After we said hello, I asked him what he was up to and he casually said that he was a sex worker now. Okay.

And then he went slightly random. "Have you ever been hit by a car, either as a pedestrian or as a bike rider?"

I told him I hadn't.

"Well, take my advice and if it ever happens to you, don't stand up."

"How do you mean?"

"I mean, I was on my bike riding home from work five years back, and some asshole in a Challenger slammed into me."

"Oh no!"

"Oh yes. And I made a fatal mistake. I tried to be Mister Manliness, so I got up off the pavement to show that I was okay. The moment I stood up, I forfeited my chance to make any insurance claim."

"Seriously?"

"Take my advice. After an accident, just lie there and be taken away on a stretcher."

"Were you badly hurt?"

"Yes. I screwed up two vertebrae and I got concussed and couldn't hang on to the bank job. I spent a year doing nothing. My personality changed too: all the things I used to care about and all the people I used to care about no longer made sense to me. I stopped hanging with my old friends and sold my guitar and kayak and made a whole new set of friends.

I still have trouble sleeping, but, you know, in a way, it feels like I've been reincarnated inside the same body."

Maybe what I need is to get hit by a Challenger. Maybe what I need is religion. Maybe what I need is to get laid. Maybe what I need is something, anything, to get me out of myself, even a pathology that makes me unique. I don't want to be dead, but I don't want to be me anymore. I've been doing that for fifty-two years and it's gotten me nowhere.

I want to reincarnate inside my own body.

21

Subway

MY NAME IS Rumwoman and I'm an alcoholic.

[*Hi, Rumwoman.*]

My real name is Julie, and last week my life had hit that point when I realized that it had been weeks since anyone had actually called me by my name, and that made me start feeling really blue, so I went to buy some rum during that crazy rainy patch we had. I met these two guys totally randomly outside the liquor store by the bus station. One of the guys was panhandling. He had a big gash in his leg above the knee that needed to be taken care of, so me and the other guy walked him to the hospital, except that on the way we ran into, like, fifty cop cars all over the place. The guy with the gash, Isaac, said, "I think they might actually be looking for me." We stopped dead, and the other guy, Ned, said, "Let's just duck into this alley for a sec."

So we went into the alley and I asked Isaac what was going on with him. He said that he had been on some meds but had stopped taking them, which is always a terrible idea—even I know that. I asked which meds, and he said it was a drug called Abilify, which was weird because I had a bunch of it in my bag. You'd be amazed how many drugs you can find, literally, on the street. When I find something, I stockpile it for moments like this one.

Ned told Isaac to wash down some Abilify with a glug from the bottle of Pinot Grigio he had on him, but Isaac refused. "I'm no alky," he said. So he ended up swallowing his Abilify with handfuls of rainwater from a puddle. Whatever gets the job done, I guess.

After Isaac took his meds, he said, "I'm actually kind of hungry. What about you guys?" It turned out all three of us were pretty hungry, so Ned said he'd go into a nearby Subway and buy us each a sub.

It's funny how specific people get with their sandwich orders, even when they're totally out of it, like Isaac was. Had to be six-inch white with ham, turkey and cheese, toasted, with pickles, black olives, pepper (no salt), lettuce and mayonnaise. Me, I can only eat a twelve-inch brown with meatballs, onions, green peppers and ranch dressing, which sounds gross but is actually really good—you should try it.

After Ned left, Isaac said that by the time he returned, the meds would have kicked in. I guess you could say we were on a winning streak. I asked him what he'd done to piss off so many cops. As you may have guessed, he was that guy who bashed his old football coach with tiki torches. Are there any cops here in the room tonight? Don't raise your hand if you are. Just remember that everything that happens in this room is anonymous. I guess if you're here, then your life is in no great shape, so who's to judge? Not me, that's for sure.

So, Ned returned with our food and we all wolfed it down, then fell into a brief, collective carbohydrate coma. Eventually I roused myself enough to fill Ned in on Isaac's crime. Ned just waggled his finger at Isaac and said, "Oh, you naughty, *naughty* boy," and we all laughed.

And Isaac's meds had finally kicked in. He said he felt like he was waking from a dream. He said it was like how you feel when you've been driving on a highway for hours and you suddenly realize you've been totally spaced out and you can't believe you haven't crashed the car. "Except in my case I did crash the car."

At that, all three of us stared at the big gash on Isaac's leg. Ned asked, "Did you get that in the fight with the coach?" and Isaac nodded.

Isaac said no way was he going to the hospital, because he'd get sent right to jail. I told him he was welcome to crash at my place if he didn't mind how small the space was. Right away he said yes. I said I also knew a doctor who was in really bad shape, but who would stitch Isaac up if we gave him a shopping bag full of oxy. I exaggerate, but you get the idea: this was going to be an expensive off-the-books surgery. Then Ned said, "Wait. The cops were after you and yet there you were, panhandling at the liquor store?"

"Totally. When you panhandle you become invisible. It's a fact."

I guess sometimes the stars just align, don't they?

To get past the cops and reach my place, we needed a disguise. Ned came up with an incredibly simple idea: umbrellas! When was the last time you saw a street person use an umbrella? It's like a cloak of invisibility or normality. A dozen cop cars passed us from all directions and didn't give us the slightest look. Ha!

My place is a rundown shithole, but that's another story. Ned left us in the lobby. He promised to check on us the next day and asked if there was anything he could bring. I requested two new pillows. I mean, where do pillows come from? Who buys pillows? They're like mushrooms or something . . . they just kind of pop up. Look, it's a pillow!

Shit, I just realized I've been speaking a long time here. I normally never talk, but how often is it that something real actually ever happens in your life? Thanks for listening.

22

Hyundai

IF I'M LUCKY I GET maybe sixty seconds after I wake up in the morning before I remember it all and my brain turns into scalding-hot shit. Yes, I'm the woman who forgot her baby in the car. Shoot me. Kill me. I could care less. It'd probably feel better than my life most of the time.

I know you want to ask me how anyone could forget their baby in a car. I'll tell you. It's easy. Your daily schedule has you on autopilot for years, and then one morning something happens to disrupt the pattern . . .

Don always dropped off Christie at day care, but he was starting to jog again that morning, so he asked me if I could do it. So Christie was in my back seat and I was driving her there when my phone rang. It was Evan from Shipping and Receiving calling about a truckload of canned goods that was delayed in western Colorado. While I was talking to him, I turned toward work instead of day care. I kept talking to him as I parked the car, got out and walked into the admin building. And then it was Adelle's birthday and so I went to Olive Garden for a group lunch, and then came five o'clock, so I went to the store down the block to buy a few

88

things for dinner. And only then did I head for my car in the parking lot.

I've listened to the recording of me calling 911. I sound insane. I was insane. I thought my daughter was dead. People from my office were huddled around trying to think of something they could do for me, but there was nothing. I was inconsolable. And then the police cars and ambulance showed up, and then a crowd of strangers gathered, making iPhone movies of it all. You should see my body language in them. It's the body language of someone who has just died inside.

Then the ambulance took my daughter away and they wouldn't let me go with her. Instead, the cops put me in handcuffs and stuck me in the back seat of their car. Neither of the cops up front would speak to me on the ride to the station, and the air conditioning was freezing. I sat there crying and shivering. Don had to find out what happened from a policeman.

The only thing that gives me mental sanctuary now is that Don came right to the station, even before going to the hospital. He ran into the interview room where the cops had stuck me and apologized to me for breaking our family routine. He got why it had happened, but the cops didn't. As far as they were concerned, I was a child murderer, and I had to agree. Even when Don called from the hospital to say that Christie was going to make it, I knew I could never forget that I had almost killed her.

All the restaurants I could never go back into. All the stores I could never shop in. The local park I could never take Christie to again. I mean, just imagine. And just imagine if she'd died. I . . . I can't go there.

Let's also discuss the in-laws who will never speak to me again and who actively campaigned for Don to divorce me. Let's discuss the social workers who came to the house every week for a full inspection and who never made eye contact with me, not so much because they despised me, but because they've seen the worst, so they didn't let themselves get invested in case I let them down. Let's discuss Don's friends, who shot these weird sideways glances at me like if they fucked me, I'd deserve it.

The only thing I could do—the only thing Don and I could think to do—was to have more kids and move far away. Once we landed, the first thing I did in the community was start an advocacy group. I know, you're wondering what I could possibly be an advocate for. It was for extended mat leave for new mothers, and I also formed a support group for new moms.

I know, barf. Trying to rebrand, but fuck you. Try nearly killing your kid because of a truckload of canned goods getting plowed into by a drunk driver outside of Fort Collins and a stupid fucking lunch with colleagues at Olive Garden. Try replaying an incredibly boring daytime work scenario over and over in your head, trying to figure out why, when I went to speak with Daria about a spreadsheet with a missing cell, I still hadn't remembered Christie in the back seat, nearly dehydrating to death. If the weather had been one degree hotter, she'd be gone.

Soon Christie will be old enough that she'll hear people whispering things about me. How do I inoculate her against those whispers? How do I make her understand that people fuck up for the most astonishingly dumb reasons? I'm not a shitty mom or even a remotely shitty human being. I just let the rhythm of life lull me into a lowered sense of alertness. Maybe that's a definition of adult life: maintaining a continual mild buzz in your head so that your daily grind doesn't bore you to death. Instead, it almost kills your kid.

23

Southwest Airlines

I'M A HEART SURGEON, a real genuine specialist, but I look like a clapped-out beef-jerky-skinned slice of crap. If you ran into me on the street, you'd look the other way. You'd never guess I was once Mr. Has-His-Shit-Together DILF. I mean, these days, if someone on a plane yelled for a doctor and I turned up, the air marshal on that flight would put me in cuffs. You know what I'd say to that air marshal? *At least I don't have to spend my entire fucking life flying on Southwest Airlines to make a living, you dumbfuck loser.* Christ, imagine sitting in gerbil-sized seats for eight hours a day, inhaling dead farts, trying to figure out if someone is in ISIS or just going insane from flying with a crap airline that is circling the drain in a competition to be the shittiest airline. Not that I have the money for a flight.

How did I end up this way? If I had to oversimplify, I'd trace it back to a bypass surgery I did maybe fifteen years ago—a pretty standard operation. But somehow, the guy woke up in the middle of it. Imagine waking up on the operating table and seeing our faces and realizing what's going on. And then . . .

And then the patient got put back under, but I could no longer view him as a generic patient undergoing a reasonably standard procedure. Something in him seemed awake, *alert*. If you eat meat (I don't anymore) and you talk to a butcher, you'll know that some cattle seem to know when they are about to be slaughtered and they send out this chemical signal and their meat flares bright red.

So that was this guy. He was asleep but he wasn't. And then something else went wrong . . . I don't even know what it was. And now the guy wasn't alert, he was gone. This was no longer a human being under my knife, nor was he/it even like a Sunday roast beef dinner. He was a chunk of *non-life*. A meteorite from five billion years ago crashing into the Arizona desert had a higher chance of containing life than this guy.

After that patient died on the table, I had to take a break from surgery. The thought of inserting a scalpel into skin suddenly made me cringe—*me*, who once enjoyed nothing more than a good high school car crash to make a Friday night in Emerg more fun. This thing called life; this thing called aliveness. What is it? At what point does being alive start and stop? You cut down a redwood and turn it into paper towels, but what about the stump? Does a little baby redwood sprout and turn into a happy new megatree? When does the tree stop living? Is it when it can no longer generate a sprout? Or in a few more decades when there's not enough DNA for scientists to rebuild extinct redwoods from scratch in a lab?

Why does life end? Once it's gone, can it return? All of us could easily kill lots of people at any time, but we mostly don't. We can take, but we can't give, except by having kids. Sex. Death. Fucking.

Eventually I became a backroom abortionist, like a throw-back from long before Roe v. Wade. I was the doctor you went to because you wouldn't or couldn't go anywhere else. It was cash only, and if you needed pain medication, I'd maybe give you something with the price marked up. But let's say I was a "real" doctor in a "real" office. How is a "real" doctor in a "real" medical practice all that different from me in my rented apartment at the back of a cucaracha's nest of a live-work dump? I offer a service at a reasonable price, and I don't think anyone ever got sepsis from me.

But stitching up wounds is still an issue for me. You don't want me stitching you up. The nurses I hire make fun of it behind my back. They call me Helen Keller. But when you're at a point in your life that you're coming to Dr. Jones, *who else are you gonna go to?*

Speaking of stitching, the other night this kid comes in. A junkie? Or maybe one of those lost souls on SSRIs? His leg was a mess from a gouge wound—the inside of it looked like red Jell-O. *Plus* it had been six hours since he'd been gashed and he hadn't gotten any treatment. There was probably pigeon shit in it by then. Or those chunks of lungs those old guys cough onto sidewalks.

Stitching him back together was like trying to sew a flank steak together with some stewing beef. I Frankensteined the whole thing. I admit I was not proud of my work, but I was coming off a bender and *who else was this guy going to go to*? I saw his face in the newspaper the next day, one of those freebie papers they leave in coffee shops. Isaac Richter. Local boy. Attacked and most likely tried to kill an old high school coach, who I'm guessing was Uncle Molesty getting his comeuppance. Ha! We're all scum.

Ah, life. We live our days. We have our memories. We have opinions. We have feelings. And they all go into a cosmic blender and become karma smoothies that get left on the counter and are forgotten. Eventually they start to get all bubbly and rotten, and then you knock yours over and it spills and stains things, but you're too lazy to wipe it up, so it turns hard, and if you neglect it long enough, it just sort of ossifies over time. And that's your legacy. You had the gift of sentience and what did it get you?

24

Tinder

M: 28

Some people shouldn't be allowed to drive. I'm thinking of those drivers who try to be super-nicey-nicey—*Hi! Look at me! I'm a nice person!*—prissy morons who leave a trail of confused and pissed-off people in their wake and, not infrequently, accidents.

What's that? I have the right of way at a four-way stop? I won't take it, because that would look greedy. Instead, I'll sit here not moving until the other person decides to go, and just then, I'll start driving and fuck things up. And then they'll yell at me, but in my heart I know I made the world a better place.

Today I screech to a halt at a four-way stop. I'm in a hurry, but I stop nonetheless, and this soccer mom in a white Toyota minivan to my right should obviously be going first, but she just sits there—so, okay, if you're that clueless, then I'll just turn left in front of you. Have a nice life, you ill-trained, useless deadweight.

I mean, what taught you to behave like such a hesitant little doormat? Was it 9/11? Was it ISIS? Was it COVID? Was it—fuck *that*. Maybe you just want to pretend you're that goody-goody woman in a sugary TV ad for some unnecessary product like air fresheners. Go for it. *Ooh! Look at me! Little twinkly stars are following me as I walk around a perfect world!*

Then I see that this useless soccer mom is tailgating me as I get on the freeway, and I feel sad that, after having been so useless, this victimy driver has decided to ride my ass as if it's going to change my mind about doormatty chimps like her. I speed away and that's that.

Me: 1

Human Race: 0

F: 34

I'm at the four-way stop when some jerk lunges into it like he has the right of way, which he doesn't, because I do. So I take my sweet time, but the sociopathic idiot turns left in front of me even though it's totally not his turn. Where do people like him get off acting like the world owes them a crown and scepter? So I follow him onto the freeway and tail him for awhile, but he's too fast for me.

°Poof°

Gone.

Jerk.

M: 28

Before I meet anyone from Tinder, I always do a real-world check to make sure they're not psycho: I put their photo into Google images to see if they stole it from someone else, and then I scour Facebook and Google for any dirt I can find.

Most of the time, I end up with a reasonably hot, slightly drunk woman, and a reasonably good lay. Of course, like anyone, I've had a few crazies I instantly ghost. "Do you want to scientifically draw my pussy before you enter it?" *Brrrrrr*. Everything is 100 percent apps, and I love eye contact and flirting. For me it's the sexiest thing of all.

So anyway, I finished doing my last-minute checks in my car out in front of the Starbucks, and then I sucked in a breath and pushed through the door.

"You!?" I hissed.

"Me? What? Wait—was that *you* driving like a jerk back there?"

"No, it was me driving like a confident human being."

"No, it was you driving like you own the road, which you don't."

"No, it was me reacting to Miss Priss taking her sweet time to exercise her right of way, so I took it for you."

"So I was a bit slow. Whoop-de-doo."

"You weren't a bit slow. You were being a hostage-taker."

"I—I what?"

"Dawdling with your thumb up your ass while you hold real drivers in real cars hostage."

"You actually think like that?"

"Don't deflect it back to me. The need to hold strangers hostage in day-to-day situations is the second-biggest indicator of psychopathy after the impulse to remove the wings from flies."

"That's absurd."

"Being a bit defensive, are we?"

"I—wait . . . you're wearing a red plaid shirt. You're the one I'm supposed to be meeting here."

"Holy shit! You're saying you're the same woman in that photo you sent me? You look nothing like your photo."

"Well, neither do you. You said you had a toned body and a swimmer's build. You look like you eat exclusively from vending machines."

"You said you were twenty-eight. There's no way you're twenty-eight."

"So I fudged it. Everyone does. You certainly do."

"Deflecting again. Nice try."

"You're probably into sick shit. I can tell."

"Can you?"

"I bet you want to get me pass-out drunk and then knife me and stuff my body into that cargo carrier on top of your car. And then you'll drive around for days knowing I'm up there, yet another one of your dead conquests."

"You're loving this, aren't you?"

"Actually—I am."

"I kind of am too."

"Tall Pike Place Roast, no sugar, no dairy?"

"Dairy? No way. Dairy is the devil."

"It *is*. I stopped eating it three months ago, and my skin cleared up and my sleep is great now."

"I can't believe you just quit dairy too."

"Look, the vegan lemon loaf is on sale."

"Sweet! I'm buying."

25

NSFL

I REMEMBER THE FIRST TIME I wondered if something fishy was going on. Wait—do I want some coffee? No. It might interfere with my meds. I'm super-clear right now, so I want to get this done before I go fuzzy again.

So, yeah, it was my junior year and I was in detention for being a wiseass in class. I was Mr. Wiseguy back then. Hard to believe when you look at me now, I know. It was just me in detention and I was reading an Archie comic, wondering why schools even bother with detentions, because they sure don't change people, just bore them to death.

So I was reading this Archie comic and Mr. Hart, my football coach, who was supervising detention, came over and sat on top of the desk in front of me, which was kind of creepy because his jock was right there inside his shorts at my eye level, and he looked at the comic and smiled. "You know, every time Archie sees Betty or Veronica he's always surrounded by cartoon hearts," he said, "but the real truth of it is that the hearts ought to be boners, because that's what's really going on there." I laughed because, I mean, it's true. He rubbed me on the back of my head and said, "Detention's over," and I said, "Yes, sir," and that's when it began.

I don't want this to sound like porn. It's so seedy, and I can't get any of it out of my head no matter how I try, and it's been over a decade now. I mean, man, how did that fucker get so inside my head? My family's pretty normal and I have a great dad, so it wasn't like I was looking for a father figure or anything. Anyway, pretty quickly, Mr. Hart became something I could never tell my father about precisely because Dad is such a great guy.

Actually, can I get a bottle of water or something? Thanks. Sorry for the hassle.

Online they use the term NSFW for things that are unsuitable to open at work, but there's another expression they have, NSFL, meaning Not Safe for Life, which flags things that you can never unsee after you see them. All my Mr. Hart stuff was NSFL. I've already said more here than I've said anywhere ever. If it wasn't for these new meds, I don't know what would have happened to me.

He did all that grooming shit with me. I got to sit beside him when we bused to games. He became friends with my folks. He shared his hotel room with me to save my parents money, he said. He was always telling me how great I was, and he listened to all my problems, and he became the closest friend you could ever hope to have. I dropped my other friends, kids my own age, because Mr. Hart said I needed to totally focus my energy on helping the team win the state championships. I was *his* quarterback.

I'm not going to share the pervy shit he did. I'll just say that the first time was in a motel in Denver where they magically only had a double bed for the two of us. And then he . . . oh man . . . he came on to me about the way in which men become champions, and the energy and responsibility they have to the other men who came before them. I fell for it. I'm not going into details. You can probably imagine. I should stop here, maybe.

How long did it go on for?

Maybe a year, until it became clear we weren't going to get to the state finals, and then he was suddenly too busy to see me. It wasn't like he was ghosting me, but all of the stuff he'd done to show me he was really my friend was just him covering his ass for when he dumped me. He knew I couldn't accuse him of doing all the shit he did. What was I going to say?

Was I planning on killing him? No. I dropped by my old high school's fair, trying to scrape a few good memories out of that dump. I was kind of doing okay, watching these two smartass kids run some kind of Lego challenge where you could win a Starbucks card. I guess I started whistling—I'm not even aware I'm doing it when I do—and one of them said, "Tuneless whistling? You know, it sounds to me like someone here got molested by their football coach." How the hell did that kid nail it? I basically lost it.

I knew where Coach Hart lived. All the shit he'd done to me during those years, how could I not? In no time I was climbing over the fence into his backyard, cutting my hands on some nails protruding from the wood, but not really feeling a thing. It was like I was a zombie in a zombie apocalypse.

Then I saw that every single item in the yard, including the pool and all the pool furniture, was still the same as it was in 2010. It felt like at any moment he was going to walk out in his bathrobe and give me a champ's massage.

You know what happened next. I'm pissed I didn't get the job done. I expected to find something sharp in the garden hut at least, but all I could find were some tiki torches.

How am I ever supposed to unsee all the shit he did to me? *Oh, be a man and get over it.* Well, it doesn't work that way. It just doesn't. Even if I had killed him, I wouldn't have been able to forget.

26

Gender Reveal Party

I'M NOT SURE IF IT was ultimately a good thing, but here's how it went down.

The four of us had been isolating for six weeks and were going squirrely like everyone else. Time dragged and then it magically sped up and then it dragged again. We basically abandoned the kids to play their brainless video games while Christian and I drank way too much. When we weren't drinking, I made lumpy sourdough baguettes and Christian locked himself in his workshop in the basement, a sort of isolation within an isolation. Families aren't meant to spend so much time together. They really aren't.

Are we nice people? Somewhat. We're not churchy or squeaky clean. We cared enough about each other at least to try to make it work. We didn't think we had any big issues to deal with, at least. My friend has a drug-addicted son who lasted about four days in lockdown before he took off. He slithered home a couple weeks later, coughing and feverish, and, of course, his family took him in and soon everyone was sick. What were they thinking? They should have locked him outside and thrown rocks at him from the windows. Instead, he got a hug and a houseful of people to infect.

Maybe if the virus had actually turned people into zombies, we could have seen the real impact. It would have made isolating feel a lot more purposeful if we were fighting off zombie hordes. Sometimes the whole pandemic felt like another Y2K. I knew people were dying, but for a long time I didn't know anyone who had. Maybe I'm retroactively justifying.

The first thing that happened to shake up our new normal was that the parents of our kids' friends bought a trampoline and posted videos of their kids having the most fun any human being has ever had at any time in human history. Our kids, Brandon and Kellie, had only ever seen trampolines on TV and were desperate to go over and jump on this one, but Christian and I said no effing way. We thought elasticized nylon trampoline material was the equivalent of an IKEA ball pit. The kids might as well go to the mall and lick the escalator handrails.

But it's all about temptation, right?

One afternoon, my best friend, Macy, was having an online gender reveal party. We've known each other since kindergarten, and I was really sad she couldn't throw a real-life celebration. I'd spent half of my isolation Zooming along with her and my Chardonnay collection. The thought of not being with her in person at this big moment was too much to bear. So . . . I told my family I needed to take a sanity walk, a long walk of at least three miles. Nobody even gave me a second glance as I went out the door.

The stroll to Macy's was nice. If I squinted my brain, I could almost pretend it was normal everyday life again. When I got to her place, she was so happy to see me. I sat in her little courtyard area with only a glass sliding door between us—much better than a computer screen, that's for sure. When she set a bottle of Pinot Grigio and a glass outside her door for me, I teared up at the sight. I poured myself a glass, then toasted her through the window, and I lost all track of time.

It turns out that while I was gone, Christian also went out for a "mental health walk." His was a booty call with his personal assistant, Janeen, who lived in a condo about a mile in the opposite direction from Macy's place. He told the kids the same thing I did: "Off to do a walk, just like your mom!"

Christian was gone for maybe ninety seconds before the kids hopped on their bikes and teleported to the trampoline. To their credit, they did stay six feet away from their friends, and took turns, but after an hour or so of bouncing, Kellie got motion sickness and had to go sit on our friends' deck until she got over it. Brandon kept bouncing and, like me and Christian, the kids lost all track of time.

Pretty much the moment the kids left, the soldering iron in Christian's workshop short-circuited and eventually set the house on fire. Ours was an old wooden house and was basically a torch. I noticed the smoke and heard the sirens as I walked home from Macy's. Brandon and Kellie caught up with me just as I rounded the corner. We saw Christian coming from the opposite direction.

The beam at the top of the staircase fell into the basement. It looked like an orange Popsicle lit from within. The four of us stood in shock as we surveyed the glowing remains.

The fire chief approached. "You the folks who live here?"

"Yes. I—yes," I said.

"All of you accounted for?"

"Yes . . . yes!"

"Were all of you out together?"

"Uh . . . yes."

"Can you tell me where you all were?"

"Out for a walk," I said.

"Okay."

Christian said, "Me too."

"It looked to me like you came from different directions."

"We didn't walk together."

"Ma'am, why do you have blue confetti in your hair?"

Christian looked at me. "You have blue confetti in your hair?"

"I was at Macy's gender reveal Zoom party. I was on the other side of a glass window the whole time!"

"Except when the confetti blew," my husband said.

"Fuck off, Christian. Where the hell were you?"

"I actually went for a genuinely real sanity walk."

The fire chief asked, "Sir, would CCTV cameras along the street confirm your story?"

Christian became flustered. "Uh, well, yes, I suppose."

"Were either of your children with you?"

"No."

I stared at them. "Where the hell were you two?"

"We went to use Sarah's trampoline."

"You *what*?"

None of us came out of this thing smelling like roses. Insurance did cover our losses, but we became the poster family for isolation-shaming on the cover of the suburb's shoppers' paper. "Local Family a Cautionary Tale for Isolation Breakers." The one good thing that came out of it was that we bought the kids a trampoline. Not much of a silver lining, but it's something.

27

Dad-Dancing

HI. I HAVE TWO KIDS: Nate, who is fifteen, and Ella, seventeen. I am a complete dad's dad. My dad bod has been sculpted by two decades of barbecues, takeout food and sleep deprivation. I make dad jokes and do all of that dad stuff that makes my kids cringe, especially when they have friends over. The kids and their friends will be downstairs listening to some boomp-boomp-boomp-bass-line modern crap music, and I'll walk in and snap my fingers. "Hey, you know, this is really cool," I'll say. "I think I can really get into this. Turn it up louder. YOLO!" And then I dad-dance while they all look on in horror.

Here's something else I do—or, at least, I did it once. Ella was having a sleepover, and she and her friends were in her room using a Ouija board. Right in the middle of what I knew was a really fraught moment ("Is the devil listening?"), I pulled the main fuse, plunging the house into darkness. You should have heard them scream! And then, when the lights were back on and they'd recovered enough to ask another question ("Evil, are you here in the room with us tonight?"), I pulled it again. Two of the sleepover guests called their parents to come pick them up early. So. Incredibly. Satisfying.

Still, I actually think that dad-dancing is my superpower. To be frank, I can't stop myself when the urge hits. A little while ago, I was coming out of a Starbucks and there was some kid—at most twenty-one?—parked in the lot in a blinged-up car with his stereo blasting that anonymous algorithm-generated boompy noise that kids have been tricked into thinking is actual music.

(Oh! Before I forget: wearing khakis with front pleats makes the whole dad-dancing thing even more powerful!)

So, as I was saying, there was this young idiot in his car outside the Starbucks. His car stereo's bass was unnecessarily loud. He looked like he was stuck waiting for someone, so I figured he was a semi-prisoner and couldn't just drive away. And I planted myself right in front of his car and started dad-dancing like *Fuck yeah! This new music you kids listen to is amazing! Bring it on! I am grooving!* I was grinding my hips. I was 1980s dancing, with swinging arms. For a full visual reference, check out Courteney Cox dancing with Bruce Springsteen in the video for "Dancing in the Dark." I'm Courteney.

Oh, to see young Dumb-Dumb's face. He was dying inside. Superpower! Passersby were enjoying my dancing, and why wouldn't they? A dad dancing his brains out amuses everyone but the young.

This kid was actually in an awkward predicament. He couldn't really get out and try to chase me away without foregrounding the lameness of his music and how ridiculous his whole cocooned nothing young life is. But here's where the situation changed in an unexpected manner: another dad-dancer soon joined me: Keith. *Keith!* He positioned himself down the sidewalk, on the other side of Mr. Bling's Blingmobile, and began echoing my moves, all in time to the Blingmobile's bass beats. It was glorious. Between us, we managed to choreograph two minutes of riveting humiliation for that young twit.

Who plans life? Nobody plans life. You try to prepare for a few things and, if you're in the right place at the right time, fortune smiles on you. And that is what happened for me and Keith. The young guy's only option was to abandon whoever he was waiting for and drive away. As Keith and I came together to give each other celebratory high fives, another car slithered up and parked in the kid's spot. It was a talent scout connected with the local TV station, who offered us a slot on the evening news if we'd dad-shame another young idiot in his car. Fuck yeah!

So that's how Keith and I formed Dad-Dancer-5000, currently the nineteenth-most-visited YouTube channel on earth. We've recruited four more dads, who, to be honest, are a bit too young and a little too fit to be total dads like me. I think they need to put on a bit more of a flesh girdle, but Ella said they were okay as they are because we needed a DILF factor. When she said this, I will admit I had to leave the room and quickly go to Urban Dictionary to look up DILF—how did Ella know a word like DILF? When I asked her, though, she just asked me what planet I live on.

This week I've been in negotiations with Hollywood, Las Vegas *and* Broadway. The universe loves Dad-Dancer-5000!

We're *The Full Monty* in pleated khakis. We have what my agent calls "authentic cluelessness," which I think is a put-down, but I don't care. And I can't believe how broad my vision has become. "Dads on Ice"! "Cirque D'ad"! Maybe a pile of *Dad* movies with Adam Sandler or Ben Stiller. They're certainly age-appropriate.

Wait.

Sorry.

Hang on a sec—I really need to take this call.

28

Laptop

I STARTED REPAIRING laptops part-time in college, and man, has it changed the way I look at humanity. These days, I prefer working with older people because I find them less scary than young people and they take everything I say as gospel—they don't argue when I say I have to take their laptop away for two or three days "to run a diagnostic." Assuming they didn't password-encrypt their files (they hardly ever do), the first thing I do is suck everything I can from their hard drive onto my own file storage system and then browse through it over lunch. If it's a man's laptop I've raided, I first look for porn, obviously. Women pretty much never have porn.

In my experience, my older male clients either have really terrible porn—tiny JPEGs and not many of them—or they have a billion images of just the craziest shit, super-organized into specific folders with super-boring folder names (Tax_files_2011_leftover), figuring that no one would ever suspect what such a file contains. Me, I suspect everything about everybody.

Sometimes the porn images are mixed in with family photos, so you go from a kid's christening to Destroying_Ashley's_Hole

113

to a summer barbecue to fecal_03_highrez886 to JPEGs of some guy washing his car. It used to freak me out that even the dullest-looking guy might have dolphin sex orgy folders on his drive (yes, that's a thing). But then, isn't that what they say about serial killers, too? You know: there's no way on earth *he* could be the one who made a delicious broth out of hitchhikers.

I've never found kiddie porn, which I'm grateful for. Curiosity can be a curse. But I can tell from some of these guys' stashes that they maybe wish they had some. I've found some bestiality, too, not just dolphins, but—I'm not going there. It's as sick as you'd think, but what am I going to do— call the cops? I would if I found some truly scary shit, I think, or kiddie porn.

The trouble is that other people's porn gets repetitive so quickly that it soon fails to register. What would be so bad that I'd call in the law? I've now reached the point where I just assume that every man has a massive porn trove inside his head as well as on his hard drive. I mean, I think about sex about 25 percent of my waking hours. And I figure so does everyone else.

My uncle works border security, and after he was put on a porn squad to track down a kid exploitation ring of some sort, he got PTSD and had to go for therapy. I guess I should find comfort in knowing that most people's porn style is pretty vanilla.

I always tell people their laptop is clean as a whistle when I hand it back. Sometimes I wonder if I should delete their porn "accidentally" while I'm repairing their laptop, but what kind of judgy statement would that be? Instead, I sometimes add images to the troves of my customers—just enough to make them go WTF? but not enough that they'd email me demanding to know if I added a four-handed massage compilation to the Thailand holiday folder they labeled Invoices_taxpaid_march2016.

There's this really good word my sister told me: "sonder." It's like "wonder" but with an "s." "Sonder" describes the moment when you're downtown and you look at all the people walking by and realize that all of them have an inner world that's as complex and fucked up and noisy as your own. The thought of all that complexity freaks you out and you have to stop thinking about it or you'll go totally nuts. That's what other people's porn does to me. It puts me in a state of sonder so extreme that I have to blank it all out and fix the graphics card or broken keypad or whatever it is that needs fixing and pretend I saw nothing.

You're likely wondering whether I ever read my customers' emails. I have, but only a few times, back when I started. People's emails are about as interesting as snatches of conversation you hear in public, things like *Barb didn't bring the onion dip to the tailgate party again this year, and I don't know how many more times I can take her "accidentally" forgetting it.* Sometimes I wondered if I should email Barb and tell her people were crapping on her reputation because of her onion dip negligence. But why bother? Barb is lazy and, I'm guessing, hates going to tailgate parties anyway.

I once read that the people to feel sorry for in life are Catholic priests because they have to sit in that weird black photo booth confessional box and listen to people hash out the same ten sins, over and over and over. If nothing else, your typical priest must spend hours trying to dream up a new sin—something, anything, to make their job more interesting.

If there were a new sin, what might it be? Ghosting people after a few bad dates? Trolling? Maybe we've already invented a new sin and just haven't realized it—something we do with our bodies and the internet? I mean, every time I go online, I feel like there's something unclean just about everywhere I go. We all do. Maybe our search histories are the eighth deadly sin. Think about it. It makes sense.

29

Karen

I'M A NICE PERSON, yes, but nice people are not necessarily good people. If you were to meet me, you might think, *Oh, that Karen is so soft-spoken and gentle. She must surely love kittens and peace and democracy.* But you'd be wrong. I don't like kittens, and I don't like blacks, and gays scare the shit out of me, especially lesbians—I mean, what's *that* all about? How did God put that 2+2 together? (Answer: God didn't.)

It's not just blacks and gays I don't like. You may as well throw in Latinos and basically anyone who's not white. And there are lots more people and things I loathe, but there are only so many hours in a day to devote to hate.

I worry that I'm giving you the wrong impression here. While I hate a lot of things, it's true, in my job as a talent scout and manager, you have to actually like the people you represent. I generally do. I especially like them when they do something weird and aren't aware of how weird they are— like Derek, the first dad-dancer. He was my biggest find. I was in a shitty mood, driving home from my older brother's second DUI hearing, and we had to stop somewhere to buy him a bus pass, of all things. I was scanning the radio, trying to find a classic rock station, and there was Derek, outside a Starbucks, doing this sphincter-clenchingly accurate imitation of Courteney Cox dancing onstage with Bruce Springsteen in the official "Dancing in the Dark" video.

I fell for Derek right then and there, which is complicated because Derek's black. So does that mean I've stopped hating black people? It's so complicated! It has to be weird for Derek or any black or gay or Latino or whoever, walking through life, knowing that behind every other smile you receive, someone wants you dead.

The thing about Dad-Dancer-5000 was that it happened so quickly. It was three weeks from spotting Derek that afternoon outside the Starbucks to booking five dad-dancers on *Jimmy Kimmel Live!* Three weeks! Looks like someone here has their shit together. [Gently puffs a breath onto her right hand's fingernails and buffs them on her sweater.]

That first wild month I doubt I slept even three hours. First I signed Derek, then his friend Keith. You may be wondering where I found three more dancers so quickly, and the answer is that I found them during a cigarette break outside a Narcotics Anonymous meeting. If you ever need to quickly recruit some human beings, I totally recommend NA meetings. Those people always need cash, and they'll sign away all rights in perpetuity just so they can back-pay a sliver of alimony. At the end of the meeting, I just said, "I need three guys who look like dads and who can dance." Presto.

I didn't make it with Derek until after we were on *Jimmy Kimmel*. We were all high on life that night, drinking champagne on other people's dimes in one of those New York hotel lobby bars with cheesy copyright-free pictures of Marilyn Monroe and Frank Sinatra bought from Costco all over the walls. Then, "Oh my Lord, it's already midnight! And we have *Good Morning America* in six hours. Bedtime for everyone!"

Derek and I ended up alone in the elevator because we were on the same floor, and that was it. And it was great, but he's so . . . *black*, and I kept being pulled in and out of being turned on by him and being surprised that I was with a black guy.

So, yes, as I said, I'm not a good person, and yet the world keeps spinning. Deal with it. And besides, the money kept flowing in, and the gigs got bigger and better. We had to re-cast two of the original NA recruits with professional dancers when they fell off the wagon again; for some people, money is a curse. I mean, for a few months there, I felt like I was a 1980s game show contestant trapped inside a plexiglass bubble in which thousand-dollar bills were flying around me and all I had to do was grab, grab, grab and all of this money was mine.

With all that cash flowing in, I could have had any rent boy or male escort I wanted. The trouble was, I was only turned on by Derek, belly roll and all. Shoot me now. So there I was, standing in the wings, all motherly and meek, telling him and the guys how terrific they all were on camera. And then, finally, I'd get to Derek's room, where he'd be on the phone with his wife or one of his kids and I had to be invisible for endless minutes while he talked about boring married shit.

Still, I had his number. After he hung up, looking guilty as only a dad's dad can look, all I had to say was something like

"Derek, I think I've figured out a new social media strategy for you" and he'd yank me onto the bed and get all black all over me.

Maybe the thing I hate the most about sex is that it always seems to make you betray yourself.

30

Taco Bell

ONE OF THE STUPIDEST things someone ever said about me being born deaf was at a wedding reception. A guest glanced my way and said to her friend, "Lucky her! It must be so peaceful inside her head." Like I can't lip-read. I grabbed a place-setting card and wrote, "I don't hear silence inside my head. I hear *nothing*."

I think she remained a completely unchanged human being, but I don't mind. You don't miss what you never had, though I think I would have learned to read and write ten times faster if I knew what these letters you see here actually "sound like" in your head.

I'm jealous that most people get to have a voice in their heads while I don't. What is it like to "talk to yourself"? What is it like to have a little angel on one shoulder, speaking into one ear, while a devil whispers in the other? Is it funny? Is it confusing? And don't get me going about music. People never stop reminding me what a loss it is not to experience it. Thanks, everyone! I'll just sit in the corner and play Bejeweled on my iPhone while you all dance.

Confession: I can sign, but I hate doing it. I can walk invisible in a crowd and no one will know I'm not like them. As soon as I sign, I look like a freak. (Yes, I know this is internalized self-hatred.) Everyone I meet feels bad because they don't know sign language, so they give me their "solidarity face" as if we were discussing the plight of the American Indian or a heap of burning koala bears.

On the other hand, all you hearing people have no idea how stupid most of you look when you dance. Men especially. They purse their lips and try to look black. It just looks dumb. Which is why Derek was a revelation. Dad-dancing changed my life. Derek made me rethink what it means to be inside my body, and I'm sorry it all blew up the way it did. It was all kind of a fluke, but how can real love be a fluke? It can't be! It's love!

I was eating Taco Bell outside the office for the 555th time because Sandy at the counter can sign and I'm too lazy to cultivate new fast-food outlets. I'd just had a new asshole ripped out of me by the temporary financial officer because I didn't get an approval from a client on storage fees in case there was a project delay, and it blew up in our faces. Boring! I think the guy just wanted to show everyone what a hard-ass he is so that he could be hired full-time. And he picks on me?

Dick.

So I was in a shitty mood, sitting on the concrete lip around the fountain, and Derek walked past. When he saw me, he noticed I didn't look very happy, so he did a mime thing. (I love mimes! They're actors who can't speak or hear!) Derek was like, "Whazzup, young lady?!"

I didn't know what to make of him. He was wearing a horrible Christmas sweater (I had no idea who he was, so didn't know this was his branding). He was just this kind of hot black dude with a dad bod who was determined to make me laugh. The thing is, for the first few minutes, he didn't know I could only lip-read him.

He worked so hard. Robin Williams came to mind. And when Derek did Courteney Cox's dance from the end of Bruce Springsteen's "Dancing in the Dark" video, I almost choked from the brilliance of it, but I still refused to laugh. I mean, this was a *dad* doing the dance, and the thing about Derek is that he understands cringe better than anyone on earth. A crowd soon gathered around our game of cat and mouse, and everyone was laughing, but not tough little me.

I finally caved when he started to do Childish Gambino's "This Is America." The crowd went wild. How often do you meet a genius? Maybe never, they're that rare.

On seeing me smile, he stopped, wiped his brow and said to me, "Young lady, you're the toughest customer I ever met."

I couldn't help myself: I had to reply in sign language. "You're the hardest worker I've ever met," I signed. He freaked out because he thought he'd disrespected my deafness, but I thought it was hilarious. He is hilarious.

We swapped phone numbers and that evening we spent three hours at the Alpine Inn Motel, and we totally rocked it.

Bonus Question: If you see a row of !!!!!!!!!!!!!!!!!!!!!!!!!!!s with no words or letters attached, what does that "sound like" inside your head?

Double Bonus Question: When you read a sentence that ends with "!" do you go back and reread it like you're shouting inside your head? And what is shouting? I know people look very ugly when they shout, so it can't be good. What is shouting!?!?!! I need to know!!!!!!!!

31

Kirkland Products

I ATTENDED AN OPTIONAL Costco employee motivation seminar because it meant thirty fewer minutes on my shift in which I had to deal with these wretched beings we have circulating through our store called customers. I'm not a people person, and I only ended up running the till at a Costco because two cashiers went on maternity leave at the same time and I happened to be the warm body holding an application form in front of him when the HR guy realized he was about to be two bodies short.

[*Fist bump*]

Part of the seminar was to try to think outside the box (Oh God, people still say this shit?) and come up with new ways of generating long-term Costco loyalty. I put up my hand. "Why not give a $500 Costco voucher to anyone who can show they legally made 'Kirkland' the middle name of their newborn child?"

Suddenly, fifteen faces were staring at me. The guy running the show said, "Chloe, that's interesting. How did you think of that?"

"How did I think of it? Um . . . with my brain."

125

"But . . ." I could tell from the guy's voice that he's done this same pep talk a zillion times and I'd come up with maybe the first plausible idea he'd ever encountered. "Don't you think that's too much money?" he asked.

"Not really. Spread that out over twenty years and it's almost zilch per year to guarantee that some kid grows up to be a permanent customer. I'll take eighty-seven beef tenderloins, thank you."

Then one of the other attendees piped up, "I don't think anyone would name their kid Kirkland. I mean, how stupid."

"I beg to differ. Haven't you noticed all those immigrant families of ten who come in here? Those parents want their kids to succeed here as quickly as possible, and one way is to give the kids names that are 1,000 percent assimilated."

"Assimi-what?"

"Totally melted into the American scene. Names like Stuart or Sarah or Greg. Not even Gregory—*Greg.*"

"That's racist."

"How is that racist? These people are here to succeed. Giving Greg the middle name Kirkland says, booyah, I'm going to college, sucker!"

Crickets.

Tumbleweeds.

Back to my till.

Soon I got a call to go to the manager's office, and I was wondering what I might have done. When I got there, Carol, the manager, asked, "Is that Kirkland middle name idea really yours?"

I was insulted. "Well, yeah. Do you think I spend my free

time visiting Kirkland brand-building online forums and ripping people's ideas off? You can give a kid as many names as
you want—there's no legal limit—so why not throw Kirkland
into the middle of the bunch? I think Prince William has,
like, twelve middle names."

"I see."

"Is there anything else you wanted to talk to me about?"

"No. Thanks, Chloe."

I went back to my station and, as I scanned flats of figs and
mega-packages of toilet paper and tube socks by the dozen,
I thought about the whole naming thing. Then I decided to
do something that, while not technically evil, would nonetheless create issues within the zealously loyal Costco community. Starting with the next customer, Elana, a mother of
five, I planted the idea of the $500 Kirkland middle-naming
program.

"Five hundred dollars? Really?"

"That's the rumor."

"Wow! Can I do it with all five kids?"

"Why not? Costco is a proud gender-neutral, family-
centered company. Five hundred bucks a kid."

"I have to talk to my husband about this."

"You do that!"

And so it went for the rest of the day. I deftly planted the
Kirkland seed with any pregnant woman and all the mothers
who came through my cash.

And then I left for the day.

The next day I was on the late shift, and soon got called
into Carol's office.

"Do you have any idea of the shitstorm you've created?"

"What?"

"Don't 'What?' me. I've just met with Legal, and we have seven people changing the middle name of their kids to Kirkland because you told them it was a thing."

Awkward pause. And then I said, "So why *can't* it be a thing?"

"What?"

"It *should* be a thing."

"I was expecting an apology."

"Give me a raise instead. I have an idea."

"I—what?"

"Is your browser open? Let me look up someone who can help us take advantage of the situation."

And that's how I met Karen, about half a year before her mega-success with Dad-Dancer-5000—talk about good timing on my part. I called her office from Carol's phone and she picked up right away. Carol, of course, was pissed because she realized that I'd just entered a new orbit and that she was now a used Kleenex in my slipstream.

Cut to three days later: local story gets picked up nationally and goes viral globally.

Cut to a year later: just over 120,000 young Americans have been christened with Kirkland as their righteous middle name. Little Kirkland license plates are now on sale at Disney World. Me? Costco's dead to me. I'm working with Dad-Dancer-5000 management now, and I'm never looking back. The moral? Sometimes employee motivation seminars really work. Man, what a shitty moral.

32

Search History

I WAS THE LAST PERSON to join the internet party, and it was not a good thing. My religion does not take a kind view of the internet. I'm not Amish or anything—technology makes America truly great. It's the things you can find on the internet that are the problem. My questionable search history started with Stormy Daniels, that woman Donald Trump paid to keep quiet about their affair. In the newspapers she looked like she could be a soccer mom, but I got to wondering what she looked like as the porn star they said she was.

So one Saturday at the library I searched for Stormy Daniels pornography, and when her titties and shaven hoohoo blasted onscreen, I felt like I was going to have a stroke. My mind couldn't even process what I was seeing, and then Clara Garfield started walking over to me from the periodicals area—probably to tell me about some dumb recipe that uses Crock-Pots—and I didn't know how to get Stormy Daniels's shorn nether bits off the screen. I panicked and lunged for the plug and yanked it out in the nick of time. I could hear my heartbeat.

What is the human heart? How does it work? Where does the devil lurk? Why does it lurk? Why do we have bodies? Why can't we just be souls?

I have never thought of myself as an easily tempted person. I got to the age of forty-four without experiencing a serious temptation. But then something broke, and I blame Stormy Daniels. After seeing those images, I spent hours looking up filthy things on the internet, there at the back of the library, with the screen facing away from the room so that I never had another life-shortening Crock-Pot moment again.

It was all such a revelation. I have only ever had sex with my husband. I raised three children, who have all turned out more or less okay. Well, two did. Laura owns a massive florist business and is poised to meet Mr. Right. Jenny's married, low-key and righteous, and already has three kids under four. Following in her mother's footsteps. Then there's Luke, who never leaves his bedroom. But he's another story.

Ken and I waited until after the wedding to have sex; the first time was on our honeymoon in Mexico, in a hotel room with no air-conditioning, after relaxing our inhibitions with some tequila and Fresca. It was certainly not a pleasurable experience, but I wanted to please my husband and have children and do my duty.

The children came almost instantly, and I was glad not to have to be intimate with Ken as often as I might have, had conception been difficult. I didn't dread sex, but pleasure-wise it rated somewhere around having to vigorously use a coal-tar shampoo to get rid of lice—just something you have to do. And frankly, it was hard to look at Ken naked. I mean, a penis is a weird thing, and I really tried never to look at his.

And then I discovered the internet. Once I started looking at naked bodies, I saw my own with new eyes. My pubic hair, for example, looked like the floor of the salon I go to. So I stood in front of my bathroom sink, debating whether to trim my hoo-hoo, but I worried that Ken would think it was an invitation. By that point, I'd seen so many penises onscreen that I couldn't map it all in my mind. But I still didn't want to see his. Ken and I had not had marital relations in many years. It didn't occur to me to wonder whether he was doing something other than praying and drinking Coors Light . . . but I'm getting ahead of myself. Anyway, I finally picked up my Lady Gillette and "trimmed my bush." (Why does anything to do with private regions sound so filthy?)

Mother of Jesus, the things people attach to their bodies and the things they put inside themselves in the name of stimulation. Is there nothing sacred? The whole porn thing is a slippery slope, and before I knew it, I was looking at grown men inserting their fists inside each other's rectums, and women sharing an enormous double-pronged dildo. I believe that's called double anal. Lord, the internet has corroded my interior world.

Out of the blue one night, while we were sitting on the couch watching a *Frasier* rerun, I asked my husband, "Ken, are you having an affair?" and he said, "Well, uh, actually, yes. I am."

"I'm not surprised. How long has it been going on?"

"Years, actually. Three? Four?"

"Anyone I know?"

"No."

I paused. "Well, it had to happen, I guess. I never thought to lose the baby fat or trim my bush for you. I guess you picked up on that, huh?"

Ken stared at me like I was speaking Chinese. "This wasn't the response I thought you'd have."

That's the moment I woke up. I think such clarity only happens once or twice in a lifetime. I didn't need to stay married to this man, whatever my church said.

Ken and I are no longer together. I don't think of him all that much, and I don't think he thinks of me, either. The divorce was like removing a Band-Aid long after the wound has healed. The two older kids were totally okay with it too. But my youngest, the one who lives in his bedroom, didn't take it well.

33

Clickbait

YOU WON'T BELIEVE!!!!!!

Has there ever been a grammatical construction that taps so deeply into the human psyche? Some people take the clickbait; some don't. My mother always takes the bait.

"You know, dear, sometimes what these websites show you is quite remarkable. I just can't believe how badly child celebrities age. It's that godless Hollywood lifestyle. They all end up looking like those pasty-faced Oompa Loompa people smoking outside of AA meetings with your Uncle Greg."

One day, for fun, I made some fake clickbait and forwarded it to my mother:

Ten Celebrities Who Eat Hamsters—Number Eight Will Blow Your Mind!
[A smiling photo of Cameron Diaz posing with a golden retriever.]

A Child Gave Halloween Candy to a Street Person. What Happened Next Will Change the Way You Live!

[Child was sodomized and then used to provoke a
pit bull fight.]

*Top Model Befriends an Anaconda. What Came
Next Will Make You Smile!*
[Anaconda quite reasonably crushes said model
to death and then swallows her whole.]

I dropped by for a visit at her place after I figured she'd
looked at them.

"Very funny, smarty-pants, very funny," she said as I came
in the door.

My mother is super-religious, but she kind of likes it
when I push her boundaries a bit. If my sisters tried it,
she'd kick them out of the family. I get to be the free-
spirited one.

On that particular afternoon, I didn't expect more than
to drink some coffee with her and then head out. I love
sitting in Mom's kitchen—it's the one place in the world
that never changes.

"How's work?" Mom asked.

"Good."

"And Hayley?" (My wife.)

"Busy. She's making a pile of costumes for Mason's
Thanksgiving pageant."

"She's so creative. You really lucked out with her."

We talked a bit about the upcoming holidays, and it was
like I was twelve again, waiting for a bowl of Campbell's veg-
etable soup and a grilled cheese sandwich. I was so happy.

Then Mom put down her coffee and excused herself to go to the bathroom. She left her laptop open.

Okay.

So.

Haven't we all wondered, even for just a few seconds, where our mothers go in the online world? Of course we have. Who wouldn't? As my mother climbed the stairs, headed for the washroom off the master bedroom, I knew I had a bit of time on my hands. So I opened Google and snooped into her search history.

felching meaning
felching m4m
felching f4m
felching drinking straw
drinking straw ocean plastics
drinking straw save turtles

[scroll]

rectum prolapse
rectum prolapse image
rectum prolapse too much sex—gay
rectum prolapse promiscuity
cbt
dildo fatigue m4m
dildo exhaustion is real?

[scroll]

walgreens discount coupon code noxema
walgreens seniors cwdes noxema
walgreens seniors codes noxema
dad dancing
dad dancing tickets
pearl necklace
figging
figging is real?
queefing

[scroll]

ryan gosling wife
ryan gosling shirtless
ryan gosling net worth
ryan gosling full frontal
kate winslet diet tips
do women cheat?
objects emergency rooms remove from butts
can fetuses have erections?
avocado texture = pleasure?
four way vs three way

"I see you've been snooping through my search history."
"Mom!!"
"Yes?"
All the love had drained from her face, and I was so frightened by the dead look in her eyes, I stuttered. "I . . ."
"Yes?"

"I . . ."

"I think you should leave now, John."

"But . . ."

"But what?"

"How could you . . . ?"

"How could I?"

"How could you look up all of this . . . this *stuff*?"

"How could I? Why shouldn't I?"

"You're . . ."

"I'm . . . ?"

"You're . . ."

"I'm a sexless old maid?"

"No!"

"Is it because my upper lip is wrinkled? Do you think I should get my lips injected with filler so I can look 'hot'?"

"Jesus, Mom, what?"

"I don't know if you should bring our savior into this."

"Jesus!"

"I just said not to bring our savior into this."

"Okay. Man. I . . ."

What to say in a situation like this? "Does Dad know?"

"Does Dad know? Why is that even a question? And why would it matter to you? Are you a tattletale? Are you a snitch? Do you snoop into Hayley's search history too? Does it arouse you?"

"Holy fuck, Mom!"

She was standing her ground, in a way I'd never seen.

She said, "Here you are thinking you're such a class clown, sending me emails with contents you think might shock me or [*air quotes; so painful*] 'freak me out.' Well, I'm not freaked out. I'm curious. I want to know what human beings are capable of. Don't you? Do you ever wonder what you're gaining or losing by living the drab little life you lead—that I lead—that all of us lead?"

Silence on my end.

"I refuse to be silent anymore. I refuse to pretend I don't know what a biracial double-anal dildo is. Don't give me that face. You know what all of this stuff is and have known for decades. But I'm supposed to live like an innocent in a nunnery?"

"No. You're right. That's stupid."

"Thank you."

A pause, and then I couldn't help myself. "But, really, does Dad know about all this?"

"Yes and no. By the way, he and I are separating."

That floored me. After a suitable silence I asked, "Mom, do you still believe in God?"

And she said, "I don't know."

34

18+

SO LAST TUESDAY NIGHT I got really hammered and decided my pubes needed shaving. What happened next is not pretty. If you're under 18, you have to stop reading here.

Now, for all you 18+ people out there, here's how it went down.

Me: F26. Were you to see me on the street, you'd think, *That young woman looks like she has her shit together. She probably has a bowl of lemons on her kitchen counter beside glass jars of interestingly shaped pasta that are stopped with jumbo corks, and fancy bottles of European bubbly water in her fridge.* But you would be wrong. I don't have my shit together.

The thing about me is that I'm hairy. Some girls are just born that way. Remember seeing the music video for that 1980s one-off hit "99 Luftballons," where the singer raises her arms and her pits look like the fringes of a clown's wig? It was such a revelation for me. I don't think I'd actually ever seen a woman with hairy armpits before. I didn't even know it was an option.

So, with my light complexion and dark hair, if I shave down there, I look like a chocolate chip cookie. It's not sexy, it's just *ick*. But after you've drunk a bottle of something Californian in the fifteen-to-twenty-dollar price range, your brain's executive functions are diminished and you can fall prey to the urgent thought: *Why have I never done a proper shaving before, like the magnificent shaving I'm about to do? My pubes need to be heart-shaped . . . that will make all the difference!*

I'm not even quite sure why it felt so urgent, but it probably had something to do with this new guy I'm sort of seeing, Jeff. He wants us to go to Burning Man, he says, but he hasn't quite committed, and maybe me having heart-shaped pubes would make him decide to go there and take me with him. Man, what a shitty excuse, but did I mention alcohol? And I'm not even sure what Burning Man is, except that it's a place where rich people get naked, do 'shrooms, blow shit up and listen to 1970s music with Google executives and don't get arrested.

Anyway, I got down to business, but given the way my bathroom is laid out, and given that I only have two small mirrors, both oval-shaped, intimate shaving was not that easy.

I was using an electric detail razor I stole from an old boyfriend, which he used for contouring his facial hair. I was feeling so artistic! When I opened a bottle of something else from Sonoma, the evening began to truly rock. I was buzzing in there like I was turning a thousand acres of Brazilian rainforest into a million hamburgers, and fuck all ecosystems. My pussy must be *radiant*.

I moved on to my perianal district. BTW, did I mention I was drunk? My small oval mirrors were useless, so I gave myself a butt shave by touch alone and I was fearless. And then my wineglass tipped over and broke, at which point I realized that I should stop. And I did.

The next morning, I woke up in a cold electric fright, the kind we all experience when we remember we drunk-dialed an ex or told our families what we really think of them or—*shaved our pubes?*

Shit . . .

I ran to the bathroom and, in the cruel light of 10:30 a.m., lifted up my T-shirt and braced for the worst and . . . okay, it wasn't that bad. A bit lopsided, and the inside of my thighs looked like Milano cookies, and I couldn't bring myself to look at my butt. Still, I would have to spend the afternoon at the waxer, getting all of this painfully fixed. Lesson learned.

And this was when my mother, with whom I'm close, phoned to say she'd just had a Japanese super-toilet installed, and would I like to come try it?

She lives only a few blocks away, so how could I say no?

Have you ever tried one of those things? They're shocking. They're *bumulous*. They get inside you and they *own* you. I closed my mom's bathroom door and enjoyed a few minutes of heaven before my sister texted to say she was PMSing and had gone shoplifting to take her mind off it and got busted stealing Reese's Pieces at Kroger, so I had to quickly say farewell to the amazing toilet. In my rush, I wasn't as hygienic as I might have been normally.

So you're wondering, *Gee, how did this all blow up?* Well, it turns out the Japanese toilet basically bit me in the ass by mixing a little bit of my poop into its jet stream and shooting it into all those raw pores. By day three, my nether regions were looking like a Hawaiian pizza. And then Jeff decided Burning Man is a go, so am I not totally stoked? No, I am not stoked. My head is buzzing from amoxicillin and I'm watching TV lying on my stomach. So, no. I. Am. Not. Stoked.

35

SPF 90

IT WAS BACK DURING that summer when it rained for three months solid and my well-meaning but slightly intrusive mother was desperate to get me out of the house. "Why on earth would you isolate yourself if you don't have to? You're young! You should be out there in the world, free to do what you want."

She had a point, but I'm not outdoorsy like my brother and sister, and I genuinely enjoy being in my room alone. My mom worries I'll turn into one of those Japanese guys who leave home for a year and then return to their old bedroom and eat ramen noodles, jerk off, play video games and never, ever, ever, ever leave home again.

Then my mother's friend Celia told her that a new reverend down at her church was stressing out over his workload. Mom, devious beast that she is, phoned him and volunteered me to work at the church every weekday afternoon from one to five.

"Thanks, Mom."

"Don't be a smartass, Jayden."

"We don't even go to church. It's hypocritical."

"It's a chance to do something for the community for once."

"For once?"

"Don't be smart with me."

"What's the pay?"

Silence.

"Oh my God, you mean it's purely volunteer?"

"Yes, it is. Would it kill you to be around people with lofty ambitions?"

"Lofty ambitions? Who's going to pay my therapy bills after the reverend molests me?"

"You start tomorrow. Any more back talk and I'm making liver for dinner for the next seven days."

And that's how I ended up walking up to the side door of the local church on the wettest day of the year, knocking on it and being let in by a smiling tubby man, the Reverend Harris, whose skin glowed so palely it seemed like it had never been touched by the sun. I mean, he was in rickets territory. I wanted nothing more than to get him some vitamin D and squeegee decades' worth of SPF 90 from his face.

"You must be Jayden."

"That's me."

"Thank you so much for coming. Your mother tells me you enjoy volunteer work and that you have a strong aptitude for service."

"Yes. I'm sure she did."

"Let me show you around."

The entire building smelled like a basement, even the third floor, where the admin office was. In the real basement, dimly lit from ground-level windows, the reverend wouldn't turn on the lights in the daytime, in order to save money on the church's energy bills. He was cheap, so cheap that when the Girl Scouts came to the door selling cookies, the reverend—or *Gerald*, as he told me to call him—told them the parish couldn't afford cookies, in the hopes that the two girls might give him some for free. But these kids are what—ten?—and it's not their decision whether to dispense free cookies to misers. When they were gone, I asked him if he or the parish was hurting for money, and Gerald said, "No, but I can buy the same kind of cookie in bulk at a Costco for two-thirds the price."

He was missing the point of a charity fundraiser.

Like any job, once I got into the routine it wasn't so bad, and I do think Gerald genuinely saw himself as a resource to help the world. His religious counseling usually had to do with marriages gone sideways, addiction, depression or loneliness. It seemed to me that he was more social worker than priest and, as such, should have been paid by the government.

When I got home each night, Mom would always ask, "Been molested yet?"

"Not yet, but tomorrow I'm leaving most of my shirt buttons undone to see what happens."

"Jayden!"

"Yeah, yeah, yeah."

My workspace was a little table in Gerald's office. My most persistent memory of him is his chalk-white face bathed in blue computer screen light. By the end of my second month, I was mostly daydreaming through my church afternoons, wondering what my upcoming senior year would be like. But eventually, the fact that Gerald was really down in the dumps penetrated even my thick teenage skin. I was sure he wasn't brooding about me going back to school and leaving him on his own again. The two of us had been polite with each other, and he was a good boss, but that was it.

One rainy afternoon, I was scanning old church documents from the 1960s and 1970s and converting them into PDFs. The rhythmic sound and light from my scanner combined with the light drumming of rain on the roof and the occasional ping of incoming texts. It felt pleasant, and I was thinking about how I'd look back on the summer as an unexpectedly good one, when I heard Gerald taking a huge gulping breath across the room. When I looked over, I saw he was crying.

I'm not good with intense emotion, but I couldn't just leave him there, so I pulled a chair over, sat down beside his desk and asked, "Hey, what's up?"

"Nothing."

"Doesn't sound like nothing to me."

"No. Maybe it really *is* nothing."

"You're losing me."

"Come here and look."

Was this going to be the moment when he showed me his dungeon orgy screen-snap compilation?

I went around to stand behind him so I could look at his screen. It was displaying a spreadsheet with colored horizontal bars filled with . . . names? . . . dates and places? "What's this?"

"That first row there—that's the people who've died of AIDS. That next line are people who died in Afghanistan. The next is filled with the ghosts of souls yet to be born."

I froze.

"I hear about dead people every day from the parishioners I counsel. Every day. I've got dozens of categories."

"I guess you would."

"Oh, Jayden." Gerald was staring at the screen, but he was really staring into infinity. "Why did we humans get stuck with being self-aware? It's a terrible, terrible thing. It's not something we wished for. Sentience got dumped in our laps, and it's not leaving. It's unfair."

"Is this like Adam and Eve, kind of? Temptation? Knowledge?"

"Jayden, boy, you don't realize it, do you?"

"Realize what, Gerald?"

"Jayden—I don't believe in anything."

"Oh. Wow. I didn't . . . notice."

"Adam and Eve? Forget eating the apple. Those two idiots should have eaten the fucking *snake*."

36

Lotto

I HAVEN'T LEFT MY BEDROOM for two years except to use the bathroom. I cut my hair when I grasp it in my hand and my ponytail feels too long. Snip. Mom stocks the mini fridge in my room with soda, and I have a kettle for ramen noodles and Cup-a-Soup. I'm twenty-three. I used to go outside, but it went bad in my head. Have you ever noticed that? How you're trying to be a part of the world and then one day you just can't do it anymore? That's me. I tried.

I was learning 3D graphics programs at the local community college, but the teacher was only one YouTube tutorial ahead of the class—you could tell. I was also taking statistics, but I'll get to that. I watch online news eight hours a day, so I know what's going on out there. And that's why I'm in here, with the windows tinfoiled and the temperature a steady 75 degrees Fahrenheit, just like a Las Vegas casino.

My mother has never *once* asked me why I stay in my room. Not once. I know I'm exploiting her maternal instincts. My dad stopped paying any attention to me pretty soon after I holed up in here, and it actually makes my life simpler. I think there's a part of him that's jealous that he can't drop out like me. In some weird, fucked-up way, I won. I figure Mom's got maybe thirty-five good years left in her, so I can pretty much stay here as long as I want.

I hear the voice inside your head asking, Does he sit in there masturbating all day? (You guessed right. I'm a he, and my name is Alex.) Or is he playing endless violent first-person shooter games? Is he writing a lame sci-fi story called something like "Droneshadow"? Is he skipping his meds? Is he one of those creepy incels the internet tells me to be afraid of? Nope to it all.

Here's what neither you nor my parents know about me: I'm rich. Last year, after taxes, I netted $1.63 million, which sits in a TD savings account earning ludicrously small amounts of interest, and I don't really care about that, because what would I spend it on anyway?

Remember the statistics course? I'm rich because I found statistical flaws in the way Dream Millions Pick Six online lotto tickets are sold. They still use a rollback deadline system, and if nobody picks all six numbers after a certain date, buying tickets in bulk is an almost certain way to rake in the bucks. It's more complicated than that—and I'm happy I don't have to go out and buy paper tickets—but that's the gist. I can't believe nobody else has figured this out. It's free money for me until they fix this loophole, if they ever do. It's crazy! But then, I haven't left my bedroom for two years, so maybe I'm the crazy one.

Why is the real world so hard to live in? All most of us do when we grow up is work for a few decades at something we hate doing until we waft away. From the perspective of continental drift or Darwinian evolution, human lives are fleeting and inconsequential, but who wants to hear a twenty-three-year-old's take on life?

I admit I'm tempted to peek out at the world now and then, through a small hole I ripped in the tinfoil over my window. There's a really cute girl who lives in the basement suite of the house next door. She was probably the quirky girl in high school; she doesn't seem to have any friends, none that I can see. I watch her come and go, though she almost never goes out anywhere. I'm wondering if she's like me—and if that's the case, then maybe I'm in luck.

I've also seen some huge dude living in the suite next to hers who's dating this really hot woman who's big like him. I think she works night shifts at a bar or something, because she always comes to visit him super-late, even after dawn. I hope they have a strong bed.

Actually, I don't even know what I mean by "late." There's no time here in my room. It could be the Mandalay Bay casino or a NORAD missile silo or a submarine inspecting the Charlie-Gibbs Fracture Zone. The only time I actually keep track is the once-weekly announcement of the ticket roll-back: Tuesdays at midnight. Within the next twenty-four hours, I usually make sixty to seventy grand.

That's a pretty good weekly paycheck, but I have to confess there's one other thing I do to make money. I shouldn't tell you what it is, because it will wreck things for me. But here goes . . .

Most people use their birth date to choose their lucky numbers, which means that, among picks, there's a massively distorted chunk of numbers between one and thirty-one. In the statistical world, we call such lottery players "birthday people," and we look down on them.

The statistical world. Like it even exists.

As a result, I always skew my numbers heavily in the thirty-two to forty-nine range. That probably earned me an extra hundred grand last year. When was the last time anyone gave you an actual way to make large amounts of money while asking nothing in return?

Wait . . . I just peeked out the hole in the tinfoil. The girl next door just left her house wearing three sweaters, even though it's hot out. Definitely someone like me. But I'm not going anywhere.

37

Gaga

BEING GAGA USED TO mean you had lost your marbles, but now it means Lady Gaga. It's kind of nice the way she rescued a word from hell like that.

Even so, "gaga" was what I heard the old-timers whispering when I walked into the country club with Dad the week he was placed on probation. He'd destroyed his tennis racket by bashing the hood of his pro's Toyota Camry with it. An onlooker described the look in my father's eyes while he was bashing away as "freaky weird and dead, like he was a salmon finally scooped into the net after a long struggle."

The first time I noticed for myself that something was amiss with Dad was at a Chinese restaurant. We ran into his friend Clive there, and Dad started to brag about his new car, and then he had to pause and ask me what kind of car it was. Only twelve months later, he didn't recognize me when I walked into his hospital room. I'm not milking this for sympathy; it was what it was. It was so quick.

Mom didn't want to discuss what had happened to Dad. He was only fifty-five when he vanished inside his head, and she was fifty-three. That's young. I was also busy with my own life. I'd had a son with Daniel, and I was drowning in new motherhood, aggravated by postpartum depression on top of it. I felt bad for my mother because she was so lonely, but I was also relieved not to have to deal with her, because she was being such a bitch. I'm an only child and, given that Dad was out of the picture and she had no friends, I'd become her only emotional focus and/or target in life. I couldn't take it. Those of you with siblings count your blessings.

The summer after Dad died, Mom invited Daniel and me and the baby for dinner. She seemed a bit rattled when she opened the door, and the house was disordered—unusual, given that she was a clean freak. After she'd settled us at the dining room table, Mom went into the kitchen and returned with plates of spaghetti sauced with heated ketchup. Daniel and I stared down in disbelief.

"I think it may not be up to my normal standard," she said. "I've not been quite myself lately."

What do you do? You put a good face on it. In hindsight we should have whisked her off to a care home that night.

In the car on the way home, I said, "Do you think what I think?" and Daniel said, "Yes."

Mom sank like a stone. I made an unexpected visit two days later, and she didn't answer the doorbell. I could hear a terrible noise inside, so I let myself in with my key. It turned out to be the smoke alarm, and there was Mom, sitting in the living room, looking puzzled at me as I raced into the kitchen. She'd left a pot on the stove that was so hot it was glowing orange. I turned the burner off and fetched a pitcher of water from the sink, then slopped it onto the pot. It hissed like a shunting freight car. That was the noise that briefly woke my mother up from her trance. It was the last time I think she was ever really her old self, and she spent it berating herself for being careless, which makes me sad. The one nice thing about the lightning-quick onset of her dementia was that she was mainly unaware it was happening. That is a blessing. I take whatever blessings I can get.

Eight months after Dad died, Mom was in the same facility where Dad had been sent, but mercifully on a different wing and floor. Neither Daniel nor I could bear to be super-valiant with Mom the way we had been with Dad. There was no point. Mom didn't recognize us when we visited, and our visits made the nurses' lives harder. Mom got much more agitated than Dad had, and she hated the baby for some reason. What are the odds of both parents getting early-onset lightning-speed dementia? I guess someone has to win the lottery.

After Mom died, people said, "Oh, I'm so sorry your mom passed that way," but what they were really saying was that they were sorry for me, the gaga time bomb. Daniel and I didn't discuss this probability outright, though we knew we had maybe twenty good years left together.

The raccoons got into the trash last night. I was in a shit-storm of a mood when I was cleaning the whole mess up, because the baby had been crying for hours. Garbage-can crap was strewn all around the front walkway, and on top of it all, it was raining. I was about to have a good little cry for myself when I saw the packaging from a genetic testing facility that Daniel had hidden inside an empty half-gallon chocolate milk carton. What were the odds of me finding that? As I age, I'm learning that pretty much everything in life is some kind of lottery, but we only remember the big payoffs, good or bad.

I searched online to see what the company tests for, and there were no surprises. No point in testing me—I'm toast—but the baby? I'll never ask, and I suspect I'll never be told.

38

Liz Claiborne Sheets

ANY SITUATION CAN BLOW UP, of course, but things blow up more in my job than in most. I'm a Canadian border security guard, and I work the crossings from Washington State into British Columbia. Already you're thinking I'm a cold, arrogant bastard who enjoys nothing more than fucking people over for no reason other than because I can—and you're absolutely right about that. But the thing you have to remember is *you people made me this way*.

I went into this job actually liking humanity, but soon found out that you people will lie about *anything*. All day, every day, all I see is liars lying to me. If that was your job, wouldn't you occasionally want to fuck people over for the fun of it?

On top of the wear and tear of all that lying, we're also bored out of our minds. At lunch we create challenges to try to keep things interesting. Maybe we'll only pull over people in red cars for enhanced screening. Or maybe it's guys with ginger beards. Maybe it's people who are too friendly. I have found that the people who lay on the charm are the ones with a hundred bucks' worth of undeclared cheese in the trunk. These are by far the funnest people to fuck over because they know darn well that they are lying and (this is critical) they also feel *actual guilt* for having done something morally wrong.

I've let people into Canada who very likely had handguns and Semtex in the trunk, but they caught me on a good day, so lucky them. At least they're lying about something cool instead of $400 worth of Liz Claiborne cotton sheets or a small piece of genuine coral for an aquarium tableau.

And you can always count your lucky stars you got me and not Judith. Judith is the most dreaded border guard of all: she's a young woman out to prove she can do the job as well as any man, like it's still 1974. Heaven help you if you end up in her lane while Brenda, the supervisor, is in Judith's booth, the two of them discussing the lunchroom's new Purell dispenser or something. You might as well turn off your ignition and put the car in park. And when you pull up, you're going nowhere except maybe the alien probe station, where we stick LEDs up your ass, looking for drugs we know aren't really there. But you actually rolled your eyes at one of Judith's questions, didn't you? She will exact her revenge for your insolence.

Last February, when my aging parents ended up in my lane at the crossing, as per protocol I had to recuse myself. Sadly for them, they ended up getting Judith . . . *and* Brenda. Perfect storm. Mom, at the wheel, kept pointing my way as if being my mother entitled her to queenly treatment—a doomed strategy with Judith. Dad, on the other hand, always disintegrates in the presence of authority figures. He'd heard about Judith from me, and when he saw her name tag, he immediately got a bad case of flop sweat. He muttered and choked out all kinds of lies. It was painful to watch—like a hot dog trying to tell you how it was made. Also, unfortunately, he'd drunk a plastic keg of raspberry Gatorade on the highway home to Canada, and badly needed to pee.

Dad managed to withstand Judith's laser-kill death eyes long enough to ask her if he could use the restroom. She said no, he'd have to wait until he and Mom cleared her station— which is actually not true. Meanwhile, Mom had decided not to declare everything she had bought in Washington State and was wearing a full-on lying face. (Ask any border guard; they're a real thing.) Dad then began whimpering about relieving himself in the empty Gatorade bottle, and when my mom screamed that he better not do that, Dad got out of the car and ran over to some shrubs on the US side. Judith and Brenda barked at him to return immediately to his vehicle, but Dad's seventy-six. What are you going to do, tase an old man to death for peeing? As he watered a rhododendron, the US code red alarms started shrieking like it was 9/11 again, and a trio of American border agents ran for him, slipping on their blue nitrile gloves as they came.

The whole thing looked kind of like the Zapruder film, with Dad ending up face down on the grassy knoll, hands cuffed behind his back. The whole border shut down. Judith, Brenda and I ran over, the ladies yelling at Dad, and me shouting at the Americans to cool their jets. A total classic donkey fuck. Long story short, Dad was convicted of inde- cent public exposure and is never allowed into the US again.

Last May my parents flew to England and were hauled in for three hours of interrogation at Heathrow. Who knows how the US border authorities have flagged Dad, but I'm pretty sure he now carries a global data stain. All because he's nervous crossing the border anyway and really needed to pee.

There's no moral to any of this except: pray to God you don't get Judith next time you go north and, really, just declare everything. Please. I want to like people again.

39

IKEA Ball Pit

IN 2003 I FLEW TO Toronto for a convention and caught SARS. I just happened to end up at the global center of it all. What are the odds? I was on a ventilator for two weeks; the virus puréed my lungs into pink cat food. I do get to tell people I'm a SARS survivor, though, which I guess is a silver lining.

Inasmuch as they can track these things, they think I contracted the virus from an escalator handrail in a downtown department store when I was shopping for shirts after my luggage got lost on my flight from Miami. A superspreader had been there at the same time as me. Four other people were infected by her, and two of them died.

At that point in my life I was exiting a bum relationship. It was humbling to lie there, drifting in and out of consciousness, and realize how few people there were who would care if I lived or died. Did I have a legacy? Had I helped anyone or anything in the just over forty years I'd been on the planet? Not really. I was employed, I paid my taxes, and now maybe I was about to die prematurely of a strange disease in a foreign country. The only interesting thing about my life would have been my death.

For six months or so after my recovery, the people where I worked were greatly relieved when I telecommuted— "telecommuted": boy, what an old-fashioned word that is. I worked from home. Home was a condominium where my neighbors avoided getting into the elevator with me. "You go ahead. I just have to get some stuff in the laundry room."

As I said, I was forty then—a very average-looking man, prematurely and somewhat harshly aged by SARS. I felt pathetically weak. I'd always used my energy to compensate for my lack of looks. Now I had neither. I'd also become germaphobic to a degree I hadn't imagined was possible.

I once read that there are only two things that guarantee a child will be successful later in life: a love of Lego and an incapacitating illness before puberty. Isn't that strange? Liking Lego just means your brain is wired well, but the illness thing I now totally get. You're lying flat on a bed or you're locked inside a germ-free room waiting for radiation treatment and— *tick, tick, tick*—you realize way earlier than most people that life is finite. How could that not affect you profoundly?

Imagine if the most you can hope for in life is not to catch a bug. I read online that the average person's lungs, spread out, would cover a tennis court. My post-SARS lungs, spread out, would maybe cover a TV screen, and they're as thick and sinewy as a catcher's mitt. The upside is that any bug trying to infect them would probably bounce right off. The downside is that I don't have that huge tennis court inside me, soaking up oxygen.

I became despondent, wondering why I should even bother with life. I'd go out of my way to touch as many public surfaces as I could: elevator buttons, hand railings, the door handles at Subway restaurants. I had to fly to my nephew's wedding and deliberately chose the cheapest airline because they never clean their seats. I mean, they say they do it once a month, but have you ever been in a plane seat that didn't have food crumbs, hairs and other kinds of DNA in and around your butt area? And those gray tubs they make you put your junk in at security are technically the most germaceous surfaces in our culture. Look it up.

The thing is, even with all this germ chasing, I never got sick. How screwed up is that? I was trying to tempt fate and . . . *nada*.

My dream experience was to roll around in an IKEA ball pit during cold and flu season. It's like the gold standard for a germ chaser, except any scenario that involved me, a single male over forty, in an IKEA ball pit would have landed me on a sex offender list.

Then I met Jody. It was late fall in 2006 and I had to go to a meeting downtown. I saw her standing by the wheelchair access button, trying to touch it with her elbow while holding a briefcase, some sort of boxed pastries and a grande Starbucks Pike Place Roast, which had to be pretty hot. I stopped and smiled. "Cold and flu season, huh?"

"Finally, someone who gets me! Can you help me out here?"

"Of course." I walked over to the oversized blue and silver button and thwacked it with my hip. The door slowly opened.

"I'm Gordon," I said.

"I'm Jody, and I love your style."

We parted ways, only to find out a few minutes later that we were attending the same meeting. Fate! During the meeting we made faces at each other, pointing at surfaces and doing "how scary out of ten?" ratings. I hadn't had so much fun communicating with anyone in years.

After the session ended, I asked, "Want to go over our notes in the restaurant?"

"Sure. And I'll bring my premoistened towelettes."

Instead, we got a room at the Hyatt the next block over, and man, it was fun. Jody took off the bedspread and did a dance of death with it, and I picked up the drinking glasses and did an improv dialogue between me and the glass: "Hi. I'm your drinking glass. I haven't been properly washed since the Kuwait War."

We got married the next month in an IKEA ball pit. It was complex to negotiate, but we got it done.

And then, some fourteen years later, COVID.

40

Bic Lighter

YOU KNOW ALL THOSE scary signs you see in mall parking lots saying VIOLATORS WILL BE TOWED? Believe none of them.

Dylan and I were at the Cineplex last week and we were standing in line when a guy drove a beautifully refinished 1968 Shelby GT500 into the parking area directly in front of the theater. He deliberately parked it diagonally across two handicapped parking spots, and then another guy in a dealership's loaner car came by and picked him up and drove him away, leaving this brightly colored hunk of injustice just sitting there. I guess the point was for the crowd of moviegoers to lust after it and stampede like elephants to the dealership, cash in hand.

Dylan looked at me and said, "I don't know about you, but I now have one raging justice boner."

"What are we going to do about this?" I replied.

We tried to elicit a bit of indignant grousing from other people in line, but all we got were things like "A dick's a dick. What are you going to do, change him? Make him atone for his crime?"

"Well, *yes*."

Pitiful stares from all directions.

I don't even remember what the movie was. Suddenly our goal was to get that fucking car towed away, preferably into the next galaxy or beyond, to punish the cheesy shit who parked it there to showcase it to upper-middle-class moviegoers.

We spoke with the theater manager. She laughed. "Oh, you activist kids. Global warming! Wealth disparity! Or whatever it is that gets you lots of social media and all that stuff. Wait: did you *buy* tickets to be here inside the theater?"

We went back outside and called the number of the towing company on the parking lot sign, and this guy with an Eastern Bloc accent picked up the phone. Dylan said he sounded like he grew up down the street from Melania Trump in Slovenia or wherever. The guy said, "We do nothing until we hear from mall management." But, of course, it was nighttime, and mall management was gone.

We were furious. How dare they! This car wasn't even electric—it was just a gas-guzzling chunk of junk from the 1960s, when cars got three miles to the gallon.

We walked over to it and had a look. To be fair (and this is really, really embarrassing to admit), it *was* a sweet-looking ride. Looking at the soft leather interior gave me a sexy lady boner, but it was justice time, not sexy time.

Then we realized we should just call the car dealership, so we did. We spoke with the late-shift manager, who said he didn't know what we were talking about (even though we could tell he totally knew).

That's when I said, "Dylan, here's when shit gets real."

I knew that for the very first time he saw something scary in my face, but I knew he was also totally turned on by it.

"Dylan," I announced, "we're having a carbecue."

I knew about carbecues because I'd read an online article on rural car torchings. There'd been a rash of them owing to fentanyl, and the fentanyl was due to OxyContin, and the OxyContin was due to political lobbying by drug companies, which was made possible because the system is set up mostly to reward lobbyists. A lobbyocracy? How fucking dismal that fentanyl is where the dream of 1776 washed ashore 250 years later. Ugh.

So we walked over to the ARCO station at the corner of the mall, which had a camping special on those white chunks of barbecue starter that smell (and probably are) totally carcinogenic. With the money I would have spent on the movie, I bought four boxes of starter, along with a long-stemmed Bic lighter.

Chances are you've never torched a vintage muscle car. To get the job done, light a box of starter and put it on top of the right front tire. To be completely sure, put a box on top of all four tires. Either way, twenty minutes later you've got yourself a party.

First, plumes of smoke rise from the tops of the four wheels. Flames start to lick the interior. And then, well past the point of no return, the engine bursts into mega-flames.

What surprises me in hindsight is that nobody bothered to call 911 until the car was about to explode.

People think I'm a cute Gen Zer, or whatever my generation

is being called this week. But I'm not a cartoon character—
my voice will be heard. I'm willing to turn this world into a
carbecue if that's what needs to be done. Things are wrong.
Things have to change.

Because Dylan and I are only seventeen, we'll be tried as
juveniles, but I want our trial to be global and as big as possible. Bring it on.

41

Dasani

I MAKE MONEY ON the side using a metal detector to search for lost objects, on beaches, mostly. But the holy grail of metal detection is to find a wedding ring, and the place to find them is beneath bridges. I actually did once find a ring on Ambleside Beach, but there was no engraving inside it. Who had owned it, I wondered? Was it lost? Was it thrown away? Either way, that little gold band had a powerful aura, like a spell had been cast on it.

I got into metal detecting five years ago, while I was in London on holiday. I was walking alongside the Thames in the eastern part of the city, and there was a guy on the bank with his detector, a bucket, a shovel and some plastic kitchen colanders. I couldn't resist going down some ancient lichen-covered steps to talk to him, and he was chatty once he knew I wasn't the competition. He told me he'd been mudlarking for some years, and my brain froze at the word. "Mudlarking." That's a thing.

Here's another fun fact I learned from him: the Queen owns not just all of the swans in the Thames, but *everything* in the Thames, including its mud. So, if you want to go muck

DOUGLAS COUPLAND | 169

about in the low tide—which is what mudlarking is—you have to write the Queen for permission. My new friend also told me, "If you had children in 1890, and they went on to become mudlarkers, it was the worst possible thing for them, because it meant they had to dig in all the raw sewage for a few lost coins or jars and pots. Once you throw something into the Thames, it's there forever. There's almost no current."

Raw sewage doesn't pour into the Thames any longer. In my friend's buckets were shards of blue-and-white pottery, some animal bones, two ancient nails and about thirty plaster tobacco pipes. "They were the cigarette butts of 150 years ago," he said. He had also found what he thought was a Roman coin, but it didn't look much like one to me. It's like when you're a kid and you're convinced every triangular rock you find is an arrowhead.

The problem with mudlarking here in North America is that it makes you realize just how few things there are to find in the sand and mud of the New World. Maybe you'll find an aboriginal middens from hundreds of years ago, but if you do, the location will become an archaeological site, which is as it should be. In the end, I think my version of mudlarking is about zoning out and making my brain go quiet while being near to nature.

A week ago, my detector bleeped around some intertidal brambles. I detected what ended up being a small, rusty bolt, but my shovel also dug up a Dasani bottle, meaning that it could only have been maybe . . . twenty years old? I noticed that there was some paper inside, so I went over to a log, sat down and unscrewed the top. I had to use a twig to remove the letter inside. It was a woman's handwriting, I figured, and the date was twelve years ago.

> Dear Future,
> Do you exist? Am I still there with you? I'm so happy today, and the world is a beautiful place for once. Whatever it is that I'm turning into, I'm going to become it as soon as possible.
> Yours with love,
> Katinka G.
> Near Cates Beach, BC, Canada

Katinka's message had traveled half a mile in a dozen years. But wait—what kind of name is Katinka? A rare enough name, for sure.

I stuck the message and bottle in the car console's drink caddy and drove to meet my hockey buddy Norm for a beer.

"Katinka?" Norm said. "I think I actually know who she is."

"What? Really?"

"Yeah, she's a bit younger than me and lived on the cul-de-sac I grew up on, in that green house with the boat out front that's been parked there forever."

I knew the house. After I left Norm, I drove to his old cul-de-sac. The boat was still there (and boy, did it need pressure washing). I parked and walked up to the front door and, fortified by beer courage, I rang the bell. A woman answered. I said, "I know this is strange, but I'm wondering if there's a Katinka who lives at this address."

The woman, Ally, turned out to be Katinka's mom. She

reminded me of someone I'd meet at my high school reunion. The stress lines on her face were those of someone my age. She told me Katinka had jumped off a bridge two years after writing the note.

"She was born sad," she said. "No, that's not fair. People shouldn't be born sad, because life will do that to them anyway."

Ally invited me in, then went to make me coffee. I looked around the living room in silence. It was so fucking depressing.

When she came back, carrying two cups of coffee, she said, "The place is dusty, I know. Please excuse it." She sat down on a sofa. "Not many visitors these days. Who am I going to have over? Someone I met on an app? The Smashing Pumpkins were right. *The world is a vampire.*"

What do you say in a situation like this? I said, "You know, Ally—I have a pressure washer I almost never get a chance to use. Why don't I come over on Sunday and give your boat a blast?"

And Ally said, "Really? Could you?"

And I said, "Yes."

42

Oxy

HAVE YOU EVER TRIED to hire a hitman? Be honest. The hardest part of it is going through your mental index of all the people you know—or barely know—and trying to choose the person who might actually know someone who will, well . . . *you* know. Wink-wink. I thought finding someone would be harder than it turned out to be, and all of that work just to get rid of my useless husband who, truth be told, ought to have been taken out a decade ago.

I know, I just used the phrase "taken out" so casually, like I'm some crime bigshot. I can practically hear you judging me. But put yourself in my shoes. I'm thirty-eight, with my only kid gone off to the next county to huff glue and make ill-advised boyfriend and tattoo choices, and . . . that's it. That's my life and legacy. Oh, and I want to start a dog grooming business to fill my days with productive labor—go capitalism! Yet there was my so-called partner, Paul, sitting at the dinner table waiting for me to feed him, all sweaty from a day at the nursery and totally uninterested in my day or funding my grooming venture.

Insider fact: Paul's underwear was always filthy because

he thought touching his own butt long enough to wash it would turn him gay. He was so unclean. After Kayella was born, he turned into Paul the Wall. He completely stopped talking, which was fine, but he earned a bundle at the nursery and wouldn't give me start-up money for my grooming business. Then he canceled our trip to Florida to see my sister, and I sat there in the TV room like a houseplant, realizing that unless I did something soon, I was going to be spending the rest of my life sitting in front of a TV like a houseplant.

Okay, in search of a hitman, I ended up going to a strip club where I knew that a friend's friend's friend's loser stepson worked as a janitor. The moment I saw him, I realized he was an easy-to-manipulate goon who'd do anything for anyone for money and/or drugs. His name was Grant.

Listen to me badmouthing young Grant like that. He might not have been a man of words, but he was a man in need of a new crankshaft for his Ski-Doo, and winter was just around the corner. Hashing out the price was a little difficult because Grant honestly saw no difference between a thousand dollars and a million dollars. Finally, I offered him three figures and when he haggled up from five hundred to eight hundred, he thought he'd gotten the better of me. I offered to throw in some oxy on top of it, and we were set. Looking back on it now, I could have paid him with Monopoly money, except he did need the cash for his crankshaft.

Right after we agreed to the price, I realized I'd be safer all around if I handed Grant oxy laced with fentanyl. Dead men can't talk, right? So I left Grant out behind the dumpster and headed for the strip club office. Please remember, I was dressed like a soccer mom, albeit one who carries a pearl-handled handgun. I barged in on the guy who runs the place, saying, "My niece ended up on a ventilator because of your nasty shit. I won't go to the cops if you hand over the rest of that batch now so no other kid out there gets hurt."

It totally worked. He handed me a ziplock bag filled with who-the-fuck-knows-what. Ciao, sucker.

FYI, killing Paul was easy. He jogged a mile every night, always along a patch of rural road that never has traffic. All Grant had to do was run Paul down at seventy miles per hour. Unimpeachable hit-and-run. While all of this was going down, I made sure to be in a Denny's with CCTVs up the ying-yang. When I left, I dropped a plastic bag with the money and drugs in the parking lot's far trash can. Ahhh . . . life was good. Paul was gone. Grant was soon to join him.

People felt so sorry for me, the poor widow!

It turned out there was way more money in the bank than Paul had let on, so:

1) I visited my sister at last,
2) I started my business, and
3) I used some of the leftover bad drugs to get rid of Kayella's wimpy tattoo artist boyfriend who, the moment he found out I had money, wanted to move in with Kayella and start giving her a full left tattoo sleeve based on those Hobbit movies.

Have you ever tried to get rid of a body? Be honest. On TV, people are always getting rid of bodies, but in real life it's hard. Your instinct is to dump it in a forest or ditch and throw some branches on top. But there are busybody joggers and smug dog walkers everywhere. So, until I think of a better solution, I bought a sporty-looking cargo carrier for the roof of my new car and stuffed the tattoo artist into it. I figure it will only buy me a little time before the raccoons try to claw their way into it—those little fuckers are smart. I'm sure I'll think of something.

43

Effexor

THIS GUY SHOWED UP at my door one afternoon holding a plastic Dasani bottle containing a note from my daughter, Katinka, who committed suicide ten years ago. He found it on a beach maybe ten miles from here. Katy took a hundred Valiums and hanged herself in the garage with a yellow extension cord. I think this guy at the door, Clem, was expecting me to be sunshine and happiness to see the bottle and the letter, but instead I felt like a bird who's flown into a window. To mask my shock, I invited him in and left him to go make coffee while he looked at all the family photos in the living room.

When I came back with the mugs, he said, "Is that her there?" He was pointing to Katy's grad photo.

I nodded. "She was happy then."

"Who's that?" He was pointing to a grad photo of Terry.

"That's my son. He died of a fentanyl OD a few months back. He was a tattoo artist."

"Oh jeez."

"You couldn't have known."

Silence.

I told Clem I was going to be frank. I admitted that Katy was a mess almost from the beginning, and I always thought it would never end well for her. She'd make friends, but she couldn't keep them. "Her mood swings were terrifying, and then some doctor put her on this crap called Effexor, which dialed down the drama for a little while," I said. "But then the drama turned into this dark, scary, gloomy crap like self-harming and cutting. I mean, what the fuck is that? I grew up on a farm. I like life when it's simple. But Katy? Imagine a roller coaster with all its cars on fire."

Clem wanted to do what a lot of people do, which is to find some comforting moral in all of it, but there isn't one for Katy—or Terry. It's nature. It's the law of averages. It's randomness. Not everyone's life has meaning. It bugs me when people try to find silver linings. I tried to get Clem to stop being such a goody two-shoes by telling him I was a pragmatist, not a moralist.

"What do you mean by pragmatist?" he asked.

"Okay, the Olympics."

"The *Olympics*?"

"Yes. I mean, why do people get so hung up about doping? You don't see those judges going apeshit when one athlete wears a springier pair of shoes than the other, do you? Springier shoes confer an artificial advantage, which is apparently no problem. But eat one poppy seed bagel and get blood-tested for opiates, and suddenly you're the devil."

"Okay . . ."

"My point is that taking steroids is no different from wearing a springier pair of shoes, so why shit on dopers? In the end, it's still the athlete's physical body that set the world record."

"They should all run barefooted, then?"

"Well, if they want to be so pure, everyone should be running naked. So, until they all do that, the Olympics is pure hypocrisy."

Clem smiled. "It would certainly make the Olympics more fun to watch."

"There you go. And while I'm at it, take vegetables. When people serve you salad, you're supposed to make a happy face and go, 'Yay, salad!' But salads often taste like crap. We've all been brainwashed into thinking vegetables are mandatory, but they're not, they're a hoax. *And*, not only that, salad greens are broad-leafed, so they soak up pesticides like sponges—Roundup and all that junk that's killing bees and butterflies and songbirds and eventually us."

"That actually makes sense."

"Thank you." I was on a roll. "Nuclear weapons."

Clem did a spit take on that one. "Wha . . .?"

"Let's be real, Clem. In the 1950s they were dropping bombs like firecrackers all over Nevada. In the casinos they'd announce the blasts so that the gamblers could go outside to view the mushroom cloud. It was fun. But if you dropped one small nuke now, people would freak out like little babies and run around suing whoever they could and, I don't know, getting hysterical thyroid cancer."

"Well, that's certainly a novel way of looking at things."

"Thank you. You know what they called seatbelts back in the 1960s?"

"No, what?"

"Sissy strips!"

Clem threw his hands up at that one and laughed.

It turns out he is a mudlarker, someone who goes trawling through mud and sand looking for, as far as I can tell, rusty nails and dead nickels. The real jackpot, he says, is usually a wedding ring. To find a message in a bottle? That choked him up. Once he started telling me this, I could see that finding Katy's message was truly important to him—it validated his hobby. While it really didn't mean much to me, he was in my house and I was the host, so I tried to be nice: "Clem, this bottle has given me a real lift."

I don't think he bought it. Still, a new look came over his face, and all at once I felt girlish and awkward there in my own living room. I looked around me. "Not many visitors these days. I mean, what's going to happen—I'm going to have someone over who I met on an *app*?" I looked into my coffee cup. "The Smashing Pumpkins were right. *The world is a vampire.*"

Clem said, "You know, Ally—I have a pressure washer I almost never get a chance to use. Why don't I come over on Sunday and give that boat in your driveway a blast?"

"It's been parked there since Ernie died," I said. "Why not?"

44

Rubbermaid Tubs

MY BIGGEST CONCERN in life is figuring out how I'm going to get to New Zealand when civilization collapses. I mean, we're in the middle of a pandemic. How unstable do things have to get before you go into survival mode and prune your earthly possessions down to what will fit into six translucent plastic tubs, each about the size of a microwave oven? My tubs are Rubbermaid, with the signature Delft-blue plastic tops that make that satisfyingly crisp burping sound when you close one after you've placed into it your essential legal documents and a 144-pack of Clif energy bars.

To other people, I look like I have my shit together, and I suppose I do. I take care of my body, and business is good. I'm a florist with good taste and an ability to maximize profits on large ordering events like weddings. I hate that I have to own a car, but what else are you going to do in our society— take a bus? But there's no way I'll own a house. Talk about an anchor. Instead, I rent, and invest my business profits into Amazon stock.

I keep my six plastic tubs in my guest room on top of the bed, all ready to go. Even before the pandemic, I never invited people over, worried they might feel uncomfortable after they saw how materially condensed my world is. My minimal furniture is rented, and so are my pots and pans. In essence, I live in a perpetual hotel room, ready to flee at any second.

What will trigger the end? Maybe, on top of the pandemic, some right-wing Proud Boy will set off a small but effective baby nuke inside Manhattan's Holland Tunnel, and there goes easy metropolitan travel for the next hundred years. There are so many other 9/11s out there in the wings, just waiting to pounce on us.

I remember the morning of the first one. I was in my bathroom, rigorously flossing to see if my gums would bleed. I was watching the mini-TV over my towel rack when *Good Morning America* cut live to downtown Manhattan. As the towers fell, I threw a bunch of shit into a suitcase (I'm embarrassed by how naive my survivalist selection was. I even threw in a can of Argentinian corned beef) and then raced to the airport. I dumped my car in the crazy-expensive day-park lot so that I could fly to—Canada? Australia? No, *New Zealand*: the gold standard of survivalist destinations, in my book.

But, of course, the sky was shut down. *Fuckers.*

I kept cycling through options in my head: Who can I bribe to get me on an Air New Zealand flight to Auckland as soon as the planes start flying again? What sort of premium would it cost me to get someone bumped off that flight? Down the road, would money even be worth anything?

I keep a margarine container full of Krugerrands in one of my Rubbermaid tubs, mixed in with a bunch of cashews so that anyone rifling through my shit maybe won't find them so easily. I'm ready to bribe like crazy. I'm maybe even ready to kill to get onto an Air New Zealand flight once shit goes down.

My sister asked me why I don't simply move to New Zealand now and spare myself the apocalyptic angst. It's a really good question. The thing is, New Zealand isn't allowing tourists in right now, and they also make immigrating kind of impossible. After all those people who made the Lord of the Rings movies there a few years back bought up the country, New Zealanders sensibly closed their gates. Big chunks of cash won't get you in the door anymore. *Fuckers*.

Needless to say, I have loaded handguns in my Rubbermaid tubs. During an apocalypse, we'll finally get to see all the guns lurking out there. You could stop making guns today and there'd be enough guns for the next ten thousand years. Gun control? That horse left the barn in 1895. For every gun you see, there are fifty thousand more hidden in church basements, in suburban attics and under the front seats of F-150s.

My sister asked what I get out of living this way, always waiting for it to happen. She also suggested that, come the apocalypse, Air New Zealand is likely to stop flying.

Who's to say she's right or I'm wrong? One day in the next few thousand years, there's going to be the last plane that ever flies. What will that plane be, and why will it be the last one? Will all the gasoline in the world be gone? Will the human race be down to the last five hundred people living on the South Island? Will the world have turned into a perpetual blizzard that has stopped planes forever?

Maybe. I like to think about that kind of stuff, because there's something about right now that I don't trust. There's something about people I don't trust. Maybe some people fucked me over in my early life. Boo-hoo, but I don't feel safe in this world.

45

CCTV

JEEZ, JUST LOOK AT my mother, with the new so-called friends she made after Dad got run over and she came into all that dough, all of them just sitting there wearing their FUCK HILLARY cardboard hats and drinking Costco cranberry juice with this weird off-brand vodka that tastes like Purell, talking about how useless men are. So then I go into the other room and they start slut-shaming women who have tattoos, which was totally *meant* for me to overhear.

I only got half a tattoo before my tattoo artist boyfriend OD'd, but it's still kind of cool—he was good at his job. It's an angel with wings, except the face is a skull, and only one wing got finished. When people see it, I can see their brains trying to figure out what's happening on my shoulder. It reminds me of this joke he used to make about dildos every time we saw someone stuffy on TV, like Nicole Kidman or the Queen. He said no matter how refined they were, if you showed any woman a dildo, they'd be wondering how it would fit inside them.

He amused me, for sure, but the clock was ticking pretty fast on that relationship. He totally cradle-robbed me, for one.

And Mom couldn't bear to look at him because she blamed him for getting me into huffing solvents, which isn't true. I actually saw something about huffing on YouTube and it made me think, *Hey, huffing solvents could be kind of fun.* Blame the internet.

I was seeing someone new, anyway: Nathaniel, who I met in the parking lot at the Brentwood Mall after a big bag of Styrofoam packing peanuts he was carrying broke open. It was just so funny. I think we picked up maybe three of them before we started laughing and couldn't stop, and then we started throwing foam peanuts at each other, and then suddenly we were at his place, which was a trailer with a really good view of the river. It's kind of like it was meant to be.

It turned out he torched cars for a living. He probably did other stuff, too, but I was never really sure.

The practical side of torching a car is interesting. To make sure it burns right down to its core, you have to place a lit box of barbecue fuel chunks on the right front tire. If you're a control freak, you do the same with all four tires, which is what Nathaniel did this one time when he took me with him. Did I mention there was a body in the car? Also, being a pro, he made sure he ground out all the serial numbers. Then he stuffed the car with the foam peanuts and crumpled-up newspapers. It was really nice, actually, bonding with Nathaniel while unfolding and crumpling a stack of papers we took from community newspaper mailboxes—ones we made sure were out of range of CCTV cameras.

When Nathaniel lit the barbecue chunks, it looked so romantic in the darkness, like candles in a swanky restaurant.

Suddenly we were having a swoony make-out session, and then *fwoomp!*

We had to get out of there really quickly, which was a bummer because it would have been so hot making it in front of a burning car, but we can't always have our cake and eat it too. Wait . . . is that the expression? Like, you can't have two good things at once?

I found my boyfriend dead on my toilet when I got home. It's sort of rude to say it, but it felt like finding a twenty-dollar bill in a jacket pocket or winning ten bucks on a lottery scratch card—which means I probably didn't love him. But you know, I'd just been huffing and was riding a high, so maybe it was the high that made me kind of heartless. I do think I'm a little bit heartless. I get it from my mom. It's her fault, actually. I'm the victim here. Wait—maybe I'm actually a hero.

46

Fentanyl

I HANDLE THE OBITUARY section of the local paper. You'd think it would be depressing, but it's not at all. I'm always dealing with people in heightened emotional states, and I enjoy being the calm one. My boss has also made it clear to me that since the obits make the paper money, my job is to subtly encourage more words rather than fewer, so I end up in a lot of intense and interesting conversations.

One of the first things I noticed when I got transferred into obits is that people often send in photos of dead men/fathers/ husbands holding up a huge fish, like a trophy salmon. Why always a fish? It drives me crazy. My sister-in-law, the hippie, said it's because, spiritually, fish represent our souls, and a man holding a trophy salmon is a man in control of his own destiny. I don't want to be sexist here, but I have yet to have anyone submit a photo of a woman holding up a fish.

I like it when people provide both a young shot and an old shot of their loved one to run together. It gives you a sense of a life's span. Why, oh, *why* do people send a photo of someone at seventy-five, when they look like a warty shrunken apple head? Is it some form of payback?

You have to submit a JPEG or fax of a death certificate before we can run your person's obit. It always pisses people off when I ask, but if we didn't do it, just imagine the prank potential. We also charge a lot. I used to get emotional when people accused me or the paper of extortion, but now it bounces right off me. In the end, it's *your* dead person, and we're the obituary section and you have no other choice.

A little while back there was this jogger who got killed in a hit-and-run. When his wife called in to place the obit, it was the only time on the job when I ever asked myself, *Did she arrange a hit?* She acted like a grieving widow, but she was chewing gum while talking (I can tell) and she addressed me like she was ordering a Subway sandwich. "I've never written one of these things before. Can you help me make it deathy but not too deathy, so people don't get bummed out? In the end, he was kind of a dick, and maybe there are some folks who'll be happy when they read that he's gone."

"Would you like a photo to run with this obituary?"

"How much is it?"

"Forty-five dollars for black-and-white and sixty-five for color."

"Do you take me for a fricking moron?"

"Ma'am, I know you're distraught."

"I'm in no way distraught, but if you're trying to tell me that in this day and age, color's more expensive to print than black-and-white, you are taking me for a fool. I'll pay forty-five for color and not a penny more."

"Ma'am, we don't negotiate. Our prices are our prices."

"Must be hard for you to get to sleep at night."

Then there are the other difficult deaths.

I've learned that whenever someone under forty dies, it's because of *an ongoing struggle*, which means either cancer or opioids. This is borderline sacrilegious, but I've noticed that people who die from a fentanyl overdose are almost always more attractive than people who die in other ways. There has to be a reason for this.

I had a fentanyl death just recently: a tattoo artist, thirty-one. His mother phoned it in, and there was a lost tone to her voice as she said, "I've been writing this obituary in my head for years."

"Ma'am?"

"He was a good kid, and then one day he wasn't."

This is the place where I know to sit back and listen. "Yeah?"

"Yeah. He wanted to be an airline pilot, and that always made me feel confident he'd do something with his life."

"Huh."

"And then he broke his shoulder painting a deck and they put him on crazy pain drugs and then cut him off, and that's when he changed—at first I thought for the better. He became a jogger. He was always down to the mill and back, his daily five miles, but I eventually figured out he only jogged to the mill to score."

Here's where I did the unthinkable. I was supposed to keep people talking, but I wasn't supposed to ask questions. "When did you figure out he was hooked?"

"Too late is when. I should have noticed earlier, but we don't see what we don't want to see. Then one evening he was over at my place watching the Academy Awards with me, and he stole all my Valium . . . not just some of it, but all of it. He wanted me to catch him. I know that now. Compared to what he was used to taking, Valium is like Pez, and it affects a different part of the brain than opioids. Last time I saw him, he was on his bike, headed to his shop. He'd just had a leaping sockeye salmon tattooed onto his left shoulder, where he'd broken it. He pointed to the moon, which was a tiny crescent, and told me we don't look up at the sky enough."

Silence. The sound of a small dog barking in the background.

"How much for two hundred words?"

"You're in luck: we have a sale this week."

47

Adderall

HAVE YOU EVER DROPPED a sock on the floor and then left it there for a few days until, finally, okay, you pick it up, and while you're doing it, you think, *Was it really that hard just to pick the damn thing up?*

Welcome to my world. Everything in my life is a sock on the floor. I spend most of my waking hours having a fascinating conversation with myself along the lines of "Pick up the sock, pick up the sock, pick up the sock . . ." But of course, the dropped sock still lies there forever.

I live in a two-bedroom rancher built for $1.95 back in the 1960s that sits in a big, weedy yard. A 2004 Pontiac Sunfire has been parked on the front lawn for a decade. It's now like a big rusty sock I can't bear to look at. So much moisture has condensed inside the car that its interior is covered in blue mold. Two years back I had an anonymous note from a neighbor asking me to do something about it, which made it all the worse inside my head. That note essentially ensured the car would never be moved.

If you drove by my place, you'd probably assume an unscrupulous female dog breeder lives here. One with a weakness for the zodiac, type 2 diabetes and a disability scooter she uses when she has to leave the house, which is almost never. Oh! And she's a hoarder, with mummified tabby cats inside all of her piles of stuff, like raisins in raisin bread. Except for the dog breeding part, you'd be right. But I didn't choose to live like this; it chose me.

Wait . . . that sounds stupid. And lazy. I'm not lazy. I swear! I just haven't been able to bring myself to pick up socks.

Until last month, when my much younger half-brother, Liam, came over with his new girlfriend, Jane. Liam works an hour away from me, developing apps, and Jane's a brand manager. If you ask me, those are very boring job titles: brand manager; app developer. Snooze. But good for him for escaping our family's multigenerational curse of failure.

I could tell Jane had been heavily primed before they arrived. When I opened the door to reveal a wall of yellowed newspapers, she didn't blink. I tried to make light of it. "I know, I'm the crazy hoarder lady with a house full of junk," I said.

But Jane replied, "No, Cory, this place is fantastic. You're unique in an era when nobody's unique. Just run with it."

That was a new response to my life. I quite liked this Jane. She went on to ask me all kinds of practical follow-up questions: How long had I been there? Was I always alone?

"I've been here since 2011. I was with Denny, but then in 2015, she was killed in a car accident."

"I'm sorry to hear that."

"I never recovered, really. And then I started collecting stuff, and I can't find the off switch."

"Huh."

Jane walked around my house like it was a museum, asking if she could touch something, or take pictures. I thought she was being very respectful, but Liam joked, "Don't be so sure about that. This time next year there'll be a hipster beer named Hoarder, and its brew pub will be a molecule-perfect recreation of your house."

I thought about that. "I'd love to go to a bar that looked like my place!"

"Then Jane's your gal."

I offered to make coffee, then caught Liam waving his hands in a no-no-no-no-no manner. But Jane said she'd love some. To be honest, my coffee isn't scary. Like many hoarders, I set aside a few dishes and some cutlery that I can find easily and that I keep somewhat clean.

To get to the point, we had a nice talk over our coffee. As Liam and Jane left, Jane gave me a pill bottle containing one blue pill. "It's Adderall. Everyone in my generation eats it like trail mix. I think you have ADHD and don't even know it. About thirty minutes after you take this, start cleaning a single room. Then write me a report about what happened and email me." She wrote her email address on the bottle with a Sharpie.

This is a woman who keeps Sharpies on her person. She is special.

The next morning, I did just what Jane told me. I woke up, made instant coffee and took the pill. A half hour later, I told myself I'd tackle the living room to try to make one room non-scary for guests. So I started . . . and suddenly I had a pile of things going out on the driveway to get hauled to the dump. This was me? Jane's drug was melting into my brain like butter into a slice of toast. For the first time since Denny died, objects no longer stuck to me like Velcro. I could look at a sock, pick it up and not think twice about it.

I was in love with a drug. Maybe you know the feeling. But I was. I felt the way I think normal people feel. Then, around midnight, I could feel it wearing off. Soon its effect was gone, like a ghost passing into a wall.

I was just stupid old me again, *but* . . . I'd been given a brief glimpse of hope. Hope!

48

Risk Aversion

ARE YOUR VEINS FILLED with ice water? Can you dump a pile of money into a stock and not look at it for months or years at a time? If you're anything like me, you're maybe three seconds away from stopping reading what I'm about to tell you. Trust me. I hate reading about money too. I know that feeling it gives you in the lower stomach: not a pukey feeling but rather an existential void fueled by every financial fuck-up you've ever experienced.

But would you continue reading if I told you this has a happy ending and you'll feel good about life at the end? If so, carry on.

Me? Male. Forty-nine. White. Middle class. Married. Two kids. Employed. Bills. Mortgage. When I was a kid, I thought I was going to be in a band and then open a restaurant that sells margaritas to dying rock stars with syphilis. Didn't happen. But at least my family eats well and I can afford to buy myself another Tommy Bahama parakeet shirt online when the first one I had sent to my office was too small for me and I was too lazy to return it.

So there's this guy named Vince. There's always "this guy

named something or other," and in my case it was Vince. It's always a friend who introduces you to a Vince. Vince doesn't make money jokes, and he has no cell phone. When you meet with him, Vince listens really well. He's totally listening to *you*. How many people do that? Vince says he is amazed to see how informed your thoughts are on oil/tech/Dubai/airlines/Scandinavia. Vince validates your own inner conviction that *you are one major player*.

You know where this is going. It's almost like Vince slipped a date rape pill in your drink, because suddenly he has an iPad and you want nothing more in the world than to PayPal him the $55,000 you'd put aside for that 1978 Corvette L48 you've lusted after since high school so he can make you instant krazy rich. Forget the Corvette—with the money you just gave Vince to put into a NASDAQ-listed rare earth mining stock out of Greenland called Ytterbex, you'll soon be in Aston Martin DB5 territory.

Okay. So. Driving home after my session with Vince, I felt like I was going to be sick and pulled the car over to the curb. All I really knew about Vince was that Kenny, my racquetball partner, said he made ten grand from Vince's tips. I swore to myself that my wife, Sadie, would never, ever, ever, ever know what I just did. I was most likely totally fucked.

I woke up after a bad sleep the next morning when the NYSE had just opened and, holy shit, Ytterbex was up 6.5 percent. WTF? I just made three grand! I went through the rest of my day with a spring in my step.

Over the next few days, the stock went up and down, but mostly up, and soon Sadie was noticing the sudden spring in my step. *I'm special! I deserve this win! I'm not at all like the other losers who don't have Vince on their side.* Speaking of Vince, on day five, with the stock now up 34 percent, I called him to ask him out for another drink. I got no answer from text, email or voice mail. But with the stock up that much, I wasn't worried.

I woke up with a peaceful, happy head. *Ommmmmm. Life is great.*

I poured some grapefruit juice and went online. Wait . . . my fifty-five grand of Ytterbex was now worth—three grand? *WTF?*

For the rest of my life, when I look back on this moment, an adrenal claw will grasp the back of my skull and I will taste acid in the back of my mouth as I relive the moment when my failure as a human being was laid bare—the moment I lost my 1978 Corvette L48.

Sadie walked into the kitchen just then. "What's up? You look terrible."

"Nothing. Just another bad sleep."

By the time I made it from the kitchen to the den, my stock had gone down to fifteen hundred. I tried to reach Vince: no such luck.

I know I promised you a happy ending, and here it is. First, Vince was arrested for trying to scam a free wide-screen TV from Walmart—the fake receipt scam. Such a cheesy crime, and fuck him. I wish I could have witnessed his handcuffed perp walk.

The same day he was arrested, China did some weird fucked-up shit and suddenly Greenland became the new rare earth metals player. Soon Ytterbex was worth 4 percent more than what I'd paid for it. I sold it pronto. I could breathe again, but I know that for the rest of my life I can never look up the value of Ytterbex again, never, ever, ever.

I escaped, but only barely. Fear and greed. Pigs get fat; hogs get slaughtered. For me, the map of the world no longer contains Greenland, and the sight of a 1978 Corvette L48 makes me look away as quickly as possible.

It's a happy ending, but I'm now damaged goods. Please, dear God, don't let Ytterbex be the next Apple.

49

Hoarding

LAST MONTH MY BOYFRIEND took me to meet his quasi-elderly lesbian half-sister, Cory, out in that part of town where you start seeing those signs advertising dew worms for sale. The house looked like its owners kept a malnourished foster child locked in a bedroom closet. Okay, that's harsh, but if you saw the place, you'd look at me and say, "Yup, Jane, you nailed it!"

Cory is a filthy hoarder. I'd never seen a hoarder except on TV, so the prospect was exciting. Before Liam rang the doorbell, he handed me a pack of Fisherman's Friend lozenges and told me to keep three of them in my mouth at all times so I wouldn't gag. I'm grateful he did.

Then he rang, the door swung open, and I tried not to look shocked. I'd never seen such a large woman. Her milk-white face was unanimated and masklike as we said cursory hellos and she and Liam chatted a little about family.

The house was filled neck-high with fantastically depressing yard sale junk. Some rooms were so jammed you couldn't even enter. All of it had been doused in cat and rat pee. It was so fucked up, it affected me the same way art does: my brain hadn't felt so stoked in years.

But I felt so sorry for Cory. Before Liam and I left, I decided to give her a twenty-milligram Adderall I had left over from last month's Starbucks trust-building workshop. It couldn't hurt her and who knows . . .

Two days later Cory wrote me an email:

Jane, that was a magic pill you gave me. I took it and, just like you said, thirty minutes later I wasn't stuck being me anymore. I was a real person who did normal things and was able to see my house for the horror show it is. I am going to ask my doctor to give me a prescription. I hope you will come for another visit to see how profoundly you have helped me.

I drove there on a Saturday morning a couple of weekends later. Liam had a lacrosse game, which he could have skipped but didn't, so I went alone.

The disgusting, rusted-out car was gone! I had to park at the curb because the driveway was filled with a massive mound of crap from inside the house. I skirted the mound and rang the doorbell. When Cory answered, she looked animated and cheerful, and not at all like the sleepwalker I'd met only two weeks back.

She showed me into the living room, which still looked scary, but at least there was a visible sofa, a chair and a coffee table.

"Cory, you've moved mountains of stuff. Way to go! And the car's gone too."

"Good riddance! And I got two hundred bucks for it."

"So, show me around."

The house was as foul-smelling as last time, but Cory's

attitude made it not seem as bad. People's moods are like light bulbs. The right one really does make all the difference.

She pointed out a desiccated rat behind a carbon-covered barbecue that was layered in stuffed toys and colored leather jackets. "I called the exterminator to come in. He took one look around and freaked, but he said that once I get rid of the junk, he'll come back. Coffee? This time we can drink it in the living room."

I will admit to almost gagging on the coffee, but I hung in. I wanted to find out more about Denny. "Is much of the stuff in the house Denny's?"

"Denny? No. She was one of those people who love empty rooms. We argued about it a lot. Before I became a hoarder, I was, I guess you'd say, a 'collector.' There was a seed there. I sometimes wonder if this hoarding is all a way of communicating with her. I believe in the afterlife, you know."

I didn't want to go in that direction. "So the Adderall is really helping you?"

"It's magic. I wish I'd known about it a decade ago."

I walked over to one of the remaining piles, figuring that the items at the bottom would have more memories attached. I pulled out a tennis racket. "This looks to be in good condition. You play?" The moment I asked the question, I felt foolish. This is a woman who retrieves her mail on a motorized scooter.

"Used to. Denny was crazy about sports. I just pretended to go along with it."

Everything had a memory of Denny attached to it, even a white plastic prescription bottle cap minus the bottle. "She was always getting sick. Most active person I ever knew, and she lived at the pharmacy."

We ordered a pizza, and after we'd eaten, we decided to empty the living room completely. The pile on the driveway got bigger, and I drove away feeling creatively satisfied. I even considered Cory a new friend.

When I got home, Liam was microwaving waffles. "Have a good visit?"

"Yeah. It was nice."

"Nothing went horribly wrong?"

I rummaged in the fridge and came up with a beer. "No. She was decisive. I was impressed."

"It'll blow up in your face at some point."

"You're so negative."

My phone buzzed at 2:03 in the morning. Cory.

"Hello?"

She was in tears.

"Cory, why are you crying?"

"We threw out the margarine tub."

I paused, then said, "We threw out quite a few margarine tubs."

"No, we threw out the one I was going to use for Denny's bird's nest. That nest was the only thing she wanted to have in the house. And I never got around to it, and now the tub is gone."

"Cory, we can find another tub."

"You don't get it. That one was *special*."

I heard cars in the background. "Cory, are you outside?"

She sniffled. "Yeah."

"Are you ripping apart the giant mound of stuff?"

"Yeah."

"Stop, okay? I'll come by tomorrow and help you find it."

"Thanks. I'll try."

After I hung up, Liam turned over and looked at me. "Told you."

50

craigslist.org

THERE IS A PERVERSE need inside all of us to have our truths heard, so here goes. It was my wedding. For once I got to rule the show, *my* show. I had a pretty good budget and a long planning window, and I'd nailed a killer venue in the last week of August. It was an old Tudor mansion that used to be a frat house until three of its aspirational members died in a gruesome hazing ritual two years back. Slam dunk. I honestly saw this as a wedding that had no possibility of cratering . . . and this wedding was *mine*.

I was aiming for about 125 guests. At that size, I could cover core family members along with my loser unlikeable relatives, but I could also invite a good number of genuine friends. Helping me in all of this was my best friend, Andrea, whom I've known since day care. To be honest, we'd never had so much fun together. She was getting married a few months after me, so we had a two-year bridezilla-fest. I wish I could take a pill that makes me feel like I am sitting in my kitchen with Andrea, a little drunk, going online to post withering anonymous critiques of other women's bridesmaid outfits.

The one person I didn't want to come to my wedding was my half-sister, Cathy, who was just like the poor, doomed spinster cartoon character Cathy, whom Gen Zers probably don't know about but can easily look up on Wikipedia. She was the focus of a three-panel cartoon that debuted in the late 1970s, a single working girl who relentlessly fat-shamed, relationship-shamed and sucked hope away from two generations of women craving female role models. The third panel was always Cathy imploding in a spasm of existential doubt that came in the form of her going "*Aaak!*"

Back to real-life Cathy: she actually got knocked up by the stick insect who ran her spin class, Lars, who fled town when he found out he was about to be a dad. When the kid, Ian, arrived, he was on the spectrum big-time. He's eleven, but he can't really talk and is terrified of everything, so he freaks out a lot. It's been really hard on Cathy, but I still didn't want to invite her, because I knew she'd bring Ian. As a kid whose entire world can go haywire if he hears the noise your car makes when you forget to put on your seatbelt, I knew he'd destroy my big day for sure.

But of course I had to invite her—family is family. And it did go horribly wrong. First, everyone there had to pretend not to gawk when Ian arrived wearing black sweatpants and a cheesy tuxedo T-shirt that had spittle down the front.

They say a wedding without a crying baby is bad luck, which is sweet—the renewing power of life! But what is not good luck is Ian, sitting in the front row between Cathy and my mother, getting stung by a bee. Hello, God, was that really necessary?

We were halfway through our vows when Ian went off like a smoke alarm. It was brutal. Cathy tried to drag him away, but the sting hurt him so much he collapsed on the ground in a ball. Cathy, my dad and my uncle had to carry him out of the wedding chapel into the rear parking lot, but we could all still hear his muffled screaming. Andrea, thank God, stood up at that point and said, "Everyone, let's take a fifteen-minute break and then come back for the rest of the ceremony."

Friends came over to me saying things like "You'll laugh about this down the road!" But no, I was never going to laugh about this, ever, and Andrea could see that, so she took me out of there to a tiny quiet closet and gave me fifteen milligrams of Valium. She is my rock. And there were maybe a dozen frat-boy spanking paddles on the wall, those wooden paddles with holes drilled into them. Great detail, God!

So then, yes, the rest of the wedding. The honeymoon. Then back to the hamster wheel of real life, still driven by a burning need for revenge. My husband told me to get over it, but I couldn't. Could you?

One day, I was randomly trawling through craigslist and somehow, in that magic internet way, I ended up on a page selling things to do with bees. I couldn't believe what I saw:

> Bee swarm. Yours for $20, but come right now.
> It's settled on a sawn branch. Bring gloves. Bees
> are peaceful creatures and are at their most
> peaceful when swarming. Namaste.

An hour later, a guy named Kyle was about to help me put that swarm in a big Rubbermaid tub. A swarm is kind of molten, and handling one is kind of like, I don't know—safe danger?

I came so close, but in the end I decided not to take the bees. Kyle did sell me five dozen pheromone sticks, though, designed to attract any swarming bees in a quarter-mile radius.

That evening I drove over to my half-sister's place when I knew she and Ian were at Very Special Aquafit. I walked around the house, tucking sticks into the gutters and on top of window ledges, turning the place into one massive bee orgy waiting to happen.

But did I throw an actual swarm into the kitchen? No, I didn't, because I'm a good person.

51

Clip Art

HERE'S A GOOD PIECE of advice for men in any social situation: never tell a woman she looks like another woman, even if she looks like Beyoncé or Giselle Bündchen. It will never work in your favor. The best you can hope for out of that situation is to end up slightly behind where you were before you said it. Another good piece of advice? Never tell a woman her dress looks good on her. Instead, say, "Wow, you're totally rocking that dress!"

On the other hand, it doesn't matter what you ladies say to a guy, because we all think we're gods.

I figured all this out through my work as a model, where I have to understand how emotion works and how we connect emotion to the hundreds of little muscles in our faces. How surfaces work, basically.

My name is Gary, but in the business I'm known as Unit—not because I'm hung like the king of Sweden, but because of what happened at a clip art shoot five years back. The photographer was a total jerk, but the gig was a killer payday. I can safely say I am one of only a small tribe of people on earth who have purchased a reasonably nice condominium solely through being a clip art model.

Clip art shoots are different from editorial or commercial work. They're done in warehouses stocked with thousands of props and garments that you have to meticulously work your way through. Here's an example: clip art with pineapples. Solo model holds pineapple and cycles through an array of responses—joy, confusion, sexiness, thoughtfulness, lottery win, gullibility and so on for a minimum of forty responses. Remember that meme a few years back about laughing women eating salad? I mean, those photos had to be created somehow.

After you do your bit, they bring in a model of the opposite sex and you do all the responses together, as well as a long extra list, like he's dumb/she's smart or "Isn't this amazing!" And then someone from another race is swapped in and it's all repeated. Next it's two guys, then two girls, and more options with mixtures of different races. All so that there are endless variations of stock shots of people and pineapples.

So, somewhere in the middle of this shoot, I made a joke, overheard by the photographer, that we should just hold out our empty hands and they could photoshop in the pineapple or pliers or dildos or whatever else. You'd think I'd just advocated for gang rape.

"You, what's your name?" the photographer said.

"Gary."

"Gary, thank you for sharing your valuable opinions about today's activities. You've given me and Ms. Dreyfus here—"

(the mousy little woman who sat in a folding chair beside him, keeping track of every cell in the shoot's spreadsheet) "—much food for thought. But until you pony up $20 million to launch your own clip art juggernaut, please keep your ideas to yourself. Now, pick up that ruby red grapefruit sliced in half and take us through the forty essential food emotions."

Dick.

Don't worry, I'm getting to how I got my nickname. But first, here's a good trick about how to get your shoulders into the right position when you're about to be photographed: 1) Raise them to your ears. 2) Pull them back. 3) Lower them. It may feel like you're going for projectile pecs or tits, but it always looks great. People look at your image and think, *Wow, that person is confident*.

Q: Are models vain?

A: Actually, genuinely vain models don't have long careers. Models who last in this business are quiet and unassuming, and treat their bodies like expensive cars. You'll never see a professional model picking blackberries (all those thorns) or near a barbecue (grease burns), and we wear gloves whenever possible.

The other thing professional models figured out long before everyone started taking selfies is that the part of your brain that looks at yourself in a mirror is totally different from the part you use when looking at a photo of yourself. With training, you can build a superhighway connection between those two parts so that you can look exactly the way you want to whenever you want to. Remember what I said about micro-emotions and the surface of your face.

I was telling this idea to Ivana, a model I've worked with for years, when that same jerk photographer barked at me, "Ah, young Gary. Putting your arts degree to good use?"

"My degree is in hotel management."

"Fantastic. Bravo."

I could tell that whatever was about to come out of that man's mouth wasn't going to be pretty.

"Gary, I think I am going to call you Unit from now on."

"Unit?"

"Yes, Unit. That's why we hired you for this series of shoots—you're a unit. You're good-looking but not too good-looking, and your face has the quality most essential for effective clip art: it's pretty much impossible to remember."

He was on a roll, and everyone in the space stopped to listen.

"If I was trying to be polite, I might say you look like the boy next door, but boys next door have something memorable going for them, like a dimple or a scar on their eyebrow." He looked at Ms. Dreyfus. "Hand sanitizer, please . . ." Ms. Dreyfus dispensed a glob and he wiped his hands. "Nature creates a unit like you so that women with extreme facial features can bring their offspring's physiognomy back into the range of what we generally consider normal. You function as a corrective measure within human biology, and there's nothing wrong with that. So, Unit, please retrieve that head of iceberg lettuce from the props wagon and pretend you're angry at it, and after that, pretend it's your enemy, and after that, look at it and give it a winning smile."

"Uhhh . . ."

"Shush. I just told you the core truth of your reason for being on earth. Thank me quickly, if you like, and just get on with your job."

"Yes, sir."

52

Nike

BE HONEST: HAVE YOU ever wandered along a beach and wanted to find a corpse washed up on the sand?

Oh, don't make that face. You know darn well the coolest thing you can possibly find on a beach is a washed-up corpse. Deep within our reptile cortexes, it's probably the dominant reason we go beachcombing in the first place. Oooh! Some pretty shells! No way. We want a *corpse*—and then the inside track on the homicide investigation.

Cut to right now.

I wanted to throw a bit of fun into an otherwise bummer museum display I was creating about the evils of marine plastics. I know: marine plastics, a total downer. Little fishy-wishies choking to death on the discarded container from your green apple–scented body scrub or the frayed ends of the Lysol wipe you wasted cleaning your dashboard because you thought you might catch something from yourself.

The display was a large tank filled with marine drift plastics. A gentle wave machine made it all move slightly. I was trying to make it look like the Pacific trash vortex, which really does put you off your dinner if you think about it too

much. The goal was to help people understand the conse-
quences of throwing something "away" by showing them
what "away" looks like. But then I asked myself, what if I
were to add a wild card to the tank to reward kids, in particular, for their attention?

To this end, I worked with Roy on the aquarium's props
team to make a fake decomposed foot in a man's size 8 Nike
sneaker. First we had to have a scientific discussion about
decomposing feet. To wit: whenever someone goes overboard
from a ship—whether a murder victim or suicide—waves bash
the body around until its appendages separate at the joints.
Most of it ends up on the ocean floor, but feet in shoes made
of buoyant synthetics float, and waves gently kiss them ashore.
In some parts of the world, especially the triangle between
Seattle, Vancouver and Victoria, finding a decomposed foot
inside a shoe on a beach is not that rare an occurrence.

When the exhibit opened, most of the people found tons
of plastics shunting together in a big lump eerily beautiful,
and yet it still activated those moral nodes of the brain that
you or I don't often use. But some of the student visitors
weren't so fascinated. So, before the next school group came
through, I hid the foot toward the north side of the installa-
tion, between a Kirin beer crate and a plastic hardhat with
Korean writing on it. And then, when I noticed them getting
restless, I said, "Hey, can any of you find the decomposed
foot in the tank?"

Talk about catnip. All of those previously bored student
visitors locked on to the exhibit in search of the Magic
Decomposed Foot. It was one of those times that made me

feel proud to be an educator. And when they spotted it, you'd think they'd found a million dollars. The one downside was that some little kids there with their parents totally freaked out and started howling. Which led to Tracy from admin coming down to give me a lecture.

"Lisa, you honestly thought this was a good idea?"

"Well, yes. Why else would I have done it?"

"We're going to have to deal with the parents of all those traumatized kids now."

"Traumatized? Don't be so dramatic. Most of the kids had a ball."

"Yes, but some didn't. Christ, I hope this doesn't make the news."

"Why does everyone coddle their kids so much? It's like parents want to SPF 100 their entire existences."

"Just get that foot out of the tank and get rid of it."

"Ugh."

"This is also going to come up at the executive meeting tomorrow, so brace yourself. The new woman running this place is a real dick."

And yes, at that meeting I got a dressing down. God, what dismal bureaucrats I work with.

But life does go on, and six months later it was summer and I was visiting friends up the coast with a place on the water. I brought along the Magic Foot, nestled it in some rocks, took a photo of it and put it on Instagram with only a geotag attached. Clean, harmless fun.

Anyhoo, not an hour after I got home, the doorbell rang, and it was the cops, who wanted to know what the foot was all about. I had to show them photos of the Magic Foot in its Nike, which settled them down. And then I asked, given all the feet that turn up on local beaches, why this was such a big deal. It turned out that a limbless torso had been found a quarter mile up the beach! Just one of those spooky coincidences, I suppose.

Except it wasn't really a coincidence. That sucker took forever to cut into chunks, and then his bits spent a week in the Thule cargo carrier on top of my RAV4, until I figured out the right way to go about getting rid of it. My solution? Hide it in plain sight while I innocently dangled my plastic masterpiece.

[Evil villain laugh.]

iPhone

YOU MAY OR MAY NOT be aware of the four kinds of suicide, but as a refresher, I'll list them here:

1. Wanted to do it and it worked.
2. Wanted to do it but flubbed it.
3. Didn't really want to do it but it happened.
4. Didn't really want to do it and nothing happened.

To this I would add a fifth kind, called "asshole." I had to deal with one of those today.

First off, I'm a cop—a good one and not a bully. Every police department everywhere has its bullies. Cops like me wish personality science could develop a bully filter so we could weed them out. Bully cops give those of us who really care about you and your world a bad name.

So, yes, I want a better world—especially one that doesn't have a Waxahachie Bridge in it. You probably have one where you live: the bridge where jumpers who really mean business go. I know of only one person who survived a jump from our bridge since it was built sixty-five years ago. That fucker is as high as the river beneath it is shallow.

When people are still on the bridge, they're jumpers. Once they hit the water, we call them lily pads. I dread being asked to go "pick a lily pad." The chief assigns that duty depending on how easy or difficult an officer has made his life since the last incident. I'm unsure if this is ethical or constitutional or an HR issue, but as a way of keeping us in line, it sure does work.

We get about twenty-five to thirty jumpers a year, an average of one every ten days. But for some reason they come in clusters, especially around the spooky juju of full moons. Whenever I notice the moon is full, I say a small prayer under my breath, and I am not a religious person. Sometimes deputations appear at city council asking the politicians to spend money on putting up anti-jumper nets, but the county's been broke since synthetic opioids burned through here in the early 2000s, so the request never makes it past the budget committee.

Okay, so now I'll get to the asshole situation. It was last Saturday at 1:30 in the afternoon. I always like Saturday shifts because during the daylight hours it's the most peaceful time of the week. (You sure don't want Saturday night duty. Saturday night weaponizes you, and I hate it. We all hate it—except the bullies.)

I digress.

I was at my desk, looking up fourteen-foot aluminum boats on craigslist, when Claire buzzed me and said, "Jumper on the Wax. The chief has chosen *you* to be today's talker-downer."

I buttoned my lip on what I wanted to say and drove out to the bridge.

It was an otherwise glorious day, that last week of spring before the mosquitoes hatch, when being able to go out in a short-sleeved shirt makes you feel good about the world. Officers Ryan and Hemphill had already coned off the bridge, and people whose cars got stuck were honking and shouting, "Jump, you fucking loser!"

I find that kind of attitude not as constructive as it perhaps could be.

As I got out of my cruiser, someone yelled, "Hey, officer, just push Sinbad off the edge!"

Sinbad. I recognized the guy. He was a Syrian refugee who'd arrived here two years back and worked at the dojo off Route 9. My forehead clenched as I tried to summon the learnings from my annual cross-cultural sensitivity training weekends.

He was up on the narrow steel guardrail, doing Cossack step dance moves interspersed with pirouettes, like he was competing on the balance beam at the Olympics. It was actually kind of awesome. And, further to the Sinbad moniker, he was holding a scimitar in his right hand—yes, a scimitar!—and an iPhone in his left, livestreaming the action.

You're livestreaming your suicide attempt? Cool dance moves be damned, you are now officially a Category Five Asshole.

But, of course, I couldn't call him out as an asshole. There's a whole de-escalation protocol you have to follow, which you've probably seen in movies—one I wish I had applied when my wife drove her Dodge Caravan into a corral full of IKEA shopping carts, or when my son filled an old microwave oven with Roman candles I'd confiscated and blew it up on the Fourth of July.

Suddenly I heard a chopper blasting toward us like we were in a Vietnam movie. At the controls was Laura, the daughter of a cop, and head of the department's aviation division. I knew from having a beer with her the night before that her Adderall dealer was out on probation, and she'd just stocked up big-time. And here she was, putting into action the idea that you can use a chopper to startle the crap out of a jumper, causing them to fall inward, away from the chopper, where I can then grab them.

There is something truly exhilarating about having a chopper come right up to your nose at a hundred miles an hour. Sinbad (actually Amir ul Zirazi) didn't know what hit him. I was able to knock the scimitar from his hand as a fellow officer, Wally, tackled him to the ground, sending the iPhone fluttering down into the Waxahachie River. And you know what he started screaming at us? "You assholes! Do you have any idea how much that phone cost me?"

Yes, the fifth mode of suicide: asshole.

54

LAN

IT WAS AN ASTONISHINGLY forgettable day—a Tuesday?— one of those days that come and go, and then at the end of your life you wonder, *Man, did I really piss away my life with an endless series of wasted Tuesdays?*

Regret: the final condiment in the meal of life.

Anyway, I was sitting in my in-home workspace, but instead of working I was actually on the Star Alliance website trying to see how I could somehow recoup my dwindling status as a 1K member, someone who flies—or flew—100,000 miles a year.

Back before everything turned to shit, being a Star Alliance 1K member was an important part of my identity. I flew about 10,000 miles a month for speeches, mostly on the topic of "How Technology Is Changing Your Life!" I'd learned that most very large companies have annual pow-wows where everyone has drinks, hooks up and bitches and moans about higher-ups. Somewhere in that mix, a speaker like me motivates your brains out.

That's not exactly true. I *can* motivate people, but usually I got hired because someone with a name like Kylie, on a corporation's entertainment committee, had to find someone to speak in the Magnolia Ballroom for forty-five minutes, someone who wouldn't actively support abortion or stringent gun control and would cost (including business class airfare and two nights in a good hotel) twenty-five grand all in. Since I tick all those boxes, I'm your man. Add those 1K member privileges—zone one boarding and lots of booze and food—and life was sweet.

Enough about that. It was an aimless Tuesday and suddenly my printer made its start-up whirring noise, except I hadn't keyed in a print command. I rolled over on my office chair and checked the LED indicator strip: *Superspreader photos.*

Right, more dismal COVID shit.

But wait—no, it was a trove of split beaver shots of Trump blackmailer Stormy Daniels. It's not like I'm some internet prig, but this was really hard-core. I quickly discerned that a neighbor had mistakenly chosen my wireless printer as his printer option and most likely had no idea. In the end, ten pages came through, and then, after a minute-long pause, the same images came through again. I'm assuming that the person behind this was wondering why nothing had printed out and pressed the same command again.

I checked my wireless preferences and saw nine different options besides my own LAN:

Orange3127
Lakeview
DeathStarzzzz
Verizon fca7%EuQ

GoDucks!
Verison5Gspeth4
Bandersnatch
Krusty
Orange4040$y77

I thought it was all pretty funny, but I didn't give it much more thought until later that evening, when I was eBaying and the printer whirred up again. I have to admit, I was curious to see what my pervy neighbor was trying to print this time. And then I did see, and it was scary—borderline illegal twink stuff, which I put directly into my shredder. Then I thought about calling the police. I went to check which servers were up and saw:

Lakeview
Verizon fca7%EuQ
GoDucks!

One of these was the perv. After a few more porn printouts over the next two hours, I narrowed the culprit down to GoDucks! But who and where was GoDucks!? The house behind me? A condo across the street? By then I just wanted to end the whole business, so I changed my router name to Heypervstopsendingillegalimagestomyprinter.

Not even one hour later, my doorbell rang. I opened the door to find a guy my age, almost a clone of myself, holding a Coors six-pack.

I said, "Oh. I'm guessing it was you."

"Yeah."

"Dude, I almost called the cops on you."

"It won't happen again."

I think he wanted me to invite him in, but no way.

"I just moved here from Orange County and it's so hard to meet people. I get desperate."

"Look, you're lucky I didn't show anyone that stuff."

"I'm sorry! I'm sorry! It won't happen again. Can you just do me a favor and change your router name back to what you used to have?"

I decided to be charitable. "Sure."

I was closing the door on him when he said, "Hey! Can I ask you to help me put a rack on my car? I just need someone to help me lift it onto my Subaru in the garage. Five minutes tops, and it's lightweight fiberglass."

I found out this guy's name was Jack and that he lived in the old Palewski house two down from me. His garage was filled with luggage tagged to a Star Alliance 1K member. As he opened the Thule cargo carrier, I asked about his own airline experiences. Chatting, he went to get something on the bench behind me, then he whacked me over the head. When I came to, I was locked inside the Thule.

I pounded, yelling to be let out. His footsteps approached.

"You know what they call people who lose their elite status memberships, don't you?"

"What? You evil fuck!"

"Fallen angels."

55

Olive Garden

OVER THE PAST SIXTY YEARS I've noticed that if you tell kids they need to live a creative life, they rarely reproduce. Instead, they spend their days trying to generate proof to demonstrate to you that they listened and are fulfilling your command to be, I don't know, a fashion designer, an app creator, a painter . . . whatever. Combine this imperative with birth control and you've got no grandchildren and no population growth. You're essentially Japan. This happened with my own two children and my friends' kids, too, and I wish I could go back in history and push a magic "undo" button.

Historically, whenever the subject of grandchildren came up, our kids, Bryanna and Duncan (twenty-nine and thirty-two), always gave my husband, Rob, and me excuses along the lines of "Yes, but not until I finish this current project."

Rob and I went along with this, but as the years passed, the issue of grandkids felt increasingly urgent. By the time they were in their early thirties, the most I was hoping for was one tiny, perfect grandchild from each of them. I guess one small source of comfort was that my brother, Nels, with his two non-reproducing kids, was in the same situation as me. At least I didn't have to look on in envy.

So, one weekend we were at a summer family picnic at my brother's, and everyone got too drunk. Some neighbors had brought their kids along, and when those families left at the kids' bedtimes, there was an awkward child-free silence out on the lawn.

I ended up sitting with Nel's daughter, Chloe, a nice enough kid, single and pretty, who began telling me about a jewelry-making program she was signing up for.

"Chloe, sweetie," I said. "Forget jewelry and all that creative stuff. Just get knocked up."

"What?"

"Absolutely. Whoever the father is, he'll usually stick around. But even if he doesn't, you've got a big family who'd happily help take care of it."

"You think so?"

"I do."

In my mind I thought I was being ironic and salty: *Good old Aunt Jane!* And Chloe was laughing as I poured myself another glass of rosé.

Her brother, Darrell, saw us laughing and came over. "What's the joke?"

"Aunt Jane says I should get knocked up."

"And Darrell," I said, "you should knock someone up too. Just have kids. The universe will take care of them."

At this point my memory gets kind of iffy, but I know I did share my theory about creativity and procreation before a sudden thunderstorm chased us all indoors.

Well, within half a year Chloe was knocked up and Darrell had knocked someone up. I was happy for them, and I honestly didn't remember giving them my tipsy advice at the summer picnic until I got a furious phone call from my brother's wife, Sheila. "I can't believe you told them to have kids!"

"I didn't tell anyone to do anything."

"That's not what they say."

Oh shit. "I believe I merely shared my theory about creativity with them."

"What are you talking about?"

So I told her.

"You think that gets you off the hook here?"

"What hook? Sheila, cool down. They're adults. They have brains. After you're twenty-one, no one can tell you to do anything you don't want to do."

"Chloe works part-time at Baskin-Robbins. Darrell just got fired from delivering SkipTheDishes, which I think means he actually got fired by a robot. How are they going to support these miraculous new beings, Miss Know-it-all?"

The call ended on a testy note, but after I hung up I realized I was jealous because Sheila was getting grandkids and I wasn't. Rob noticed I was acting strange and asked what was up. I said it was nothing, but the jealousy began to eat me up and I realized I had to do something about it. So one morning I got in the car and drove to Bryanna's sound mixing studio (she's a sound editor: creative!) and suggested the two of us go to a surprise lunch.

"What's up?"

"Nothing," I lied, though I know I sounded jittery.

We went to an Olive Garden by the highway off-ramp.

Once we were seated, Bryanna asked, "Mom, what's going on? Do you have bad news?"

"No. It's just that . . ."

"What?"

"I'm sorry I told you that you should be creative when you grew up."

"Huh? I thought you were going to tell me you had cancer or something."

"No. I just wanted to say that it was a bad idea to tell you to follow a creative path."

"I—I don't know what to say. What on earth happened to trigger this? I mean—what the actual fuck?"

"Don't use vulgar language."

Coffee arrived and we ordered food I had a hunch would go uneaten. Then I explained my theory, and before she shot it down, I asked Bryanna to think of all of her friends who were in similar child-free boats.

"This is so presumptuous, Mom, I don't know where to begin."

"Humor me."

"Does Dad know about this idiotic theory?"

"I haven't really shared it fully with him."

"Fine. I'm going to leave this restaurant right now and call him and tell him I think you have dementia."

"Okay. Do that. But I still want grandkids."

And off she went, salad uneaten.

—

Bryanna's due next month. She's not married, and she's mostly not talking to me, but I don't care because I know she'll want a free babysitter. I still think I should never have encouraged her to take piano lessons. Or dance class. Or anything else.

Heed this warning.

56

Dipping Sauce

HI, I'M SHARON AND I work as a dietitian for a large American hospital chain. Here's a story for you. In 1983, America entered a perfect food storm set off by McDonald's introduction of the Chicken McNugget, a white-meat finger food served alongside an array of high-fructose corn syrup–based dipping sauces. McNuggets tapped all dimensions—psychological and gastronomical—and were an instant and massive success. Most Americans have happy Chicken McNugget childhood memories.

But the success of the McNugget came with a shadowy cost: not only did it inadvertently help fuel the country's type 2 diabetes epidemic, it also created millions of tons of unusable, unsellable chicken wings. These un-Nuggetable wings went to the landfill. Imagine thousands of garbage trucks swarmed by millions of skreeing seagulls eager for a taste of gelatinous decomposing wing. I don't mean to get poetic, but the sheer biological mass of it all amazes me. Hundreds of millions of people eating a lot of anything is pretty scary. Every massively popular food comes with significant and frightening biological side effects.

The second factor that created the early-1980s perfect food storm was the drinking laws in America's northeastern states. In order for bars to be open at happy hour between five and seven p.m., the bar needed to serve some kind of food to soak up the underpriced happy hour booze. Enter some unsung hero out there in Boston or Providence or Bangor, who thought about those tens of millions of unwanted, un-loved chicken wings and said to himself/herself: *You know, technically, legally, if pressed, you could actually view these surplus wings as . . . food.*

Soon people no longer viewed wings as something dis-gusting to be trucked to the landfill. Wings became Buffalo wings! Cajun wings!

"Honey, what's that wing recipe of yours that everybody loves?"

I mention all this to explain why, after I began my research into the history of fast-food chicken in America, I became a vegetarian. And why, though everyone in my family loves chicken wings, I refuse to buy them or cook them or do any-thing with them. I mean, just look at them. They're gross: pink and goosebumpy and kind of fetal.

The irony is that part of my job is ordering food in bulk. On any working day I may order three thousand beef hearts, eight hundred pounds of liver and a mile of hot dogs made from a wide range of body parts like urethras and fallopian tubes, ingredients that would make even a cat-food producer cringe.

One day it got to me. I clicked the return key to order one ton of reticular beef tripe (a honeycombed entity that comes from a cow's second stomach chamber), then sat back in my chair and confessed to my assistant, Azita, that I was going to ask to be reassigned.

"Sharon, ordering tripe is spooky even at the best of times," she replied. "Order some vegetables. That's what I do when I get trapped down a meat hole."

"Somehow I don't think even that will fix my brain."

"Then have some of my carrot sticks. I chopped them fresh this morning."

"Thanks."

My husband, Taylor, and my sons, Taylor Junior and Brandon (fifteen and seventeen), were perplexed when I told them I was going vegetarian. Taylor Junior said, "Sharon, are you turning into a fifteen-year-old girl? You're the queen of the four food groups. If you don't eat meat, aren't you being kind of hypocritical, considering your job?"

"I'm applying for a transfer."

"*What?*" My husband has been unemployed since COVID.

"I'm not quitting. I asked to be moved elsewhere in the hospital."

"So, Mom, does this mean you're going to stop cooking meat?"

"I suppose I can still cook it, but I don't think I can taste-test it while it's cooking."

My gag reflex soon informed me that, no, I couldn't cook meat. Even the thought of meat sharing the same shelf as my vegetarian options in the fridge soon weirded me out. Taylor and the boys tried to be okay with my choice, but after my first few attempts to make tasty vegetarian fare (mostly macaroni), they began to get testy. I found myself ordering Uber Eats to deal with the family's different menus, but that was expensive, so not a long-term strategy.

And then it was Super Bowl Sunday. Taylor's friends usually come over in sports jerseys and turn the TV room into a beer garden. The food is traditionally, almost superstitiously, guacamole, onion chip dip and massive trays of takeout Cajun wings from the bar on the corner. Even when I was a meat-eater, I usually avoided the whole event and went over to my friend Diane's place, where we would knit and watch a romcom. But I had a cold and was feeling draggy, so I stayed upstairs, bracing myself for the onslaught of walrusy woo-hooing.

Eventually I heard the doorbell ring, and I knew it was the delivery guy bringing the four massive trays of Cajun wings. Shortly afterwards, I heard a tremendous crash from the kitchen. I ran downstairs and found Taylor's friend Norm on his back, giggling—he was drunk—and the four trays of fallen wings, which had shat out their contents in all directions. Wings were glued to the cabinet doors, the walls, the chairs, my windowsill succulents, the stove. Norm looked like a zombie who had just feasted on a family of five.

Taylor helped him up and told him to strip down to his gonch. He pushed Norm into the half bath to wash off, and fetched him a pair of his old sweatpants and a T-shirt. Then my husband actually looked at me and asked, "Hon, could you take care of this mess? We're just at the start of the third quarter."

At that moment, a wing came unstuck from the fridge and splatted onto the floor.

"No," I said, and I grabbed my purse and got into my car and checked into a motel a few miles away.

I don't know what to do. But I'm not sure I can go back.

57

Using

ONE DAY MY MOTHER was normal and then she wasn't. Two years ago, she came home from work one night and announced that she was becoming a vegetarian. A week later, she went full vegan and soon she had moved out of the house into a monthly rental place. I soon learned that when you tell your friends that a woman over thirty has gone vegan, they assume she's coming out as lesbian, which wasn't the case with Mom. (Although it would be nice for her to have someone, anyone, in her life.)

What makes Mom's transformation so weird is that she was kind of an old-fashioned TV mom who worked as a dietitian for a big hospital chain. When I was little, it was like the four food groups were always seated at the dinner table like invisible themed mascots.

I think I'm closer to my mother than most guys are, though she was always cool with me or my brother asking her questions. When I wanted to know why she had changed food gears twice, she said, "First I couldn't eat anything that was once a body—an organism with bilateral symmetry—which meant no animals. But then I was cleaning out the fridge and

there was a milk carton at the back that I'd somehow over-
looked for months, and when I poured it into the sink it was
a gray-blue color and I realized I couldn't eat anything that
came *from* a body either."

After she left home was when I started using.

Someone at the clinic tried to tell me that I was being
juvenile and using drugs to punish my mother for becoming
a weirdo, but that's lame. I love my Mom and I don't trust
any guy who doesn't feel the same about his mother. It's like
a litmus test for detecting damaged men. Try it sometime.

But yeah. Me using stuff? That surprised me, too. I thought
I liked myself, but apparently I don't. I mean, we're the ones
stuck inside our bodies, so you'd think it'd be way easier to
understand yourself and to refrain from doing anything so
destructive. But it isn't. Instead, you have to go to rehab,
where you're stuck with thirty other people who are all
trapped inside their bodies just like you. And just like you,
they've lost the ability to know themselves. Or at least that's
the impression I came away with.

Why be so weird about food? Why get into drugs? And
also, why sex? After Mom left, my dad almost immediately
turned into a horndog glued to Tinder. I still haven't told
Mom about that, nor will I.

My younger brother became orthorexic, which is kind of
like anorexia in that it indicates a damaged relationship with
your body. (Yes, I speak like a rehab person, but humor me.)
Instead of not eating at all, you start eating only skinless
chicken breasts, protein powders and steamed vegetables;
instead of going for a jog, you run marathons and live at the

gym. You also pull away from people and the world. It's anorexia in disguise.

People say quitting drugs is just mind over matter, but they're not the ones stuck inside a body starving for a drug that is scientifically known to be 1,000 percent addictive. Some people are also more prone to addiction than others. That would be me. I've actually never tried cigarettes or booze because I know it would be a one-way street. And I don't know if I'll ever be truly free from meth, or the drugs I used that led to my meth addiction.

I was a lone user. I'm the one whose face you see in the obituaries looking way too young. I don't yet have the missing teeth and facial sores of a meth-head. I think I got off the bus in time—I won't ever get that bad—but I know a few people who didn't. Their faces now look like chew toys, and they'll likely be dead within a year.

When Mom moved out, I became the family's official problem, maybe so we wouldn't have to discuss her being gone.

When you heard the word "rehab," you probably assumed my family's loaded. Ha. Mom works, but Dad's been unemployed for years. All of my family's savings ended up going to New Promises. They likely financed the repaving of the rehab center's outdoor smoking area, along with the huge dreamcatcher they hung in the entry lobby, where they admit you after taking away everything you brought with you. And then you sit around with people who, like you, are thinking of drugs every waking moment. I hate myself for doing this to my family. I really do.

I was released a day earlier than expected and nobody was there to pick me up. My phone was dead, so I ended up hitchhiking home, which took maybe six hours. When I walked into the house, nobody was home. It was the saddest, quietest moment of my life.

In the kitchen, I poured myself a glass of water and, as I drank it, I stared at the windowsill where Mom's succulents were dying from neglect. I gave them half of my glass of water, and suddenly I had the shivers. There we were, me and a few plants, sharing a holy bond of aliveness, both of us needing care and also needing to give care.

I gathered all the succulents together in a cardboard box and called a taxi. And then I went to see my mother, as though for the first time since I was a child.

58

Starbursts

I USED TO BE A COP, but four years ago, during that big cold snap, I severed my Achilles tendon chasing a methhead over a chain-link fence. All that time I spent getting my badge, followed by fifteen years on the force, and my sergeant is like, "Dan, would it kill you to do desk duty for awhile?"

"Actually, yes, it would. I like being out in the world. Sitting in a chair all day, filling out forms, is a living death."

When he wouldn't give an inch, I did desk duty for a little while. And then I quit and became the same thing that all cops who quit early do: a private detective.

Being a private dick mostly involves sitting in a car all day, staking out houses or mailboxes, waiting for people who pretty much never show up. But at least I make a $500 per diem. You need to know that about detectives: everything costs you $500. Me answering the phone will cost you $500, and me sitting in my Challenger for a day will cost you $500 plus expenses. If you like getting paid handsomely for doing fuck all, then this gig's for you. Forget driving for Uber or all that twenty-first-century gig shit.

Before I'll work for you, I have to interview you. Why? Because how do I know *you're* not the psycho? Maybe you're a stalker and you want me to help you raise your game.

I have three basic kinds of jobs. First, following people who are making personal injury medical claims. I usually end up filming them lifting heavy things into the beds of their trucks. Second, trying to find people who don't want to be located, which, thank you Facebook and internet, is almost impossible these days. Third, trying to catch a good old-fashioned cheating spouse.

Catching cheating spouses in the act is the most profitable gig, because the client is going crazy with suspicion and jealousy, so you can tack on all kinds of fees to your basic rate and they'll say, "Yeah, yeah, yeah—just nail that bitch/bastard."

In general, cheaters are very lazy. Nine times out of ten I just have to stake out a motel parking lot. But one day last year, when I was sitting in a lot, I was startled by a knock on my car window. It was a woman who clearly matched the photo my client had given me of his wife, Mrs. Kerry-Ann Knox. She was smiling, which I thought unusual.

"Yes, it's me. And I'm not the psycho one."

I was flustered at being made. "I'm—that obvious?"

"I can't imagine what Kevin's paying you for all of this, but your car looks pretty expensive. I love the color, by the way."

She complimented my car! I already liked her way better than her creepster husband. "Uh, thanks. Red's always been my favorite."

"Me too. In college I had a red Ford El Camino."

"Wow! I used to have an El Camino. What year?"

"Seventy-seven."

"That's a classic. You've got good taste."

"I had to sell it after college and it almost killed me. I loved that car."

"You can always get another one."

"I know, but at my age it'd look like I borrowed it from my kid."

"I sometimes go to the car shows down in Arizona, which are filled with 1970s muscle cars. And every single guy there—"

"No women, I'm guessing."

I smiled. "Nope. All the men are exactly my age, and we're all lusting after the cars we couldn't afford in high school. I felt like some kind of punchline."

"Good taste is never a cliché. How long have you had this Challenger?"

"Almost a year now."

"And?"

"And it totally hauls ass!"

"What's the fastest you've taken it?"

"I, uh . . ."

"Come on. How fast?"

"On the straight stretch down by the water, I got her up to 140."

"Booyah!"

"But don't tell anyone. I don't want them to know I red-lined it when I trade it in."

"Your secret is my secret. Oh—are those Starburst fruit chews on the seat beside you?"

"Only the finest."

"Can I have an orange one? I have coffee breath and it's grossing me out."

I reached over and removed two orange Starbursts from the pack. "Take two, on the house."

"You're a lifesaver." She opened one, popped it into her mouth and started chewing. Then she said, "Make sure you bill Kevin a few hundred for the candy."

"You know how this works?"

"I looked up the cost of hiring someone to follow Kevin a few months back. The way you guys bill is insane."

"We're not regulated."

"You certainly aren't. It almost got me wondering if I should get into the business."

"Don't! It's so boring, you wouldn't believe it. The past three minutes have been more interesting than the past four years combined."

"You sweet-talking devil, you." She paused and stared for a moment at the door to room 106. "So, you're probably wondering why I'm in a motel parking lot at . . ." she looked at her iPhone, "2:47 on a Wednesday afternoon."

"I, uh . . ."

"I'm here meeting my ex-husband, Reid."

"You have an ex?"

"I got married when I was sixteen."

"That's legal?"

"It was a different era, and it didn't last long. I never told Kevin."

"Oh."

"There's more . . ."

"I'm listening."

"I'm helping Reid become a woman."

I snorted. "Holy fuck."

"He'll make a good woman! I swear!"

"I don't doubt you." I popped a Starburst myself. Banana. "Man, this is sort of like that old movie, *Breakfast at Tiffany's*, where it turns out Holly Whatshername has a secret hillbilly husband."

"You've seen that? It's kind of how I feel with Reid and Kevin."

"I admit I kind of liked it."

"Wait—that's like the song lyric based on the movie, you know?" And she hummed it: *"Breakfast at Tiffany's . . . We both kind of liked it . . ."*

We were married within a year and now we run stings together. We're a crime-fighting duo, and you know what? Life rocks. Booyah!

59

DUI

I DROVE TO PATTI'S in a fog. Two hours before, I'd plowed my FJ Cruiser into the side of a Windstar minivan driven by a soccer mom with two kids in car seats in the back. The kids were okay, but the soccer mom was in intensive care. Technically it was 100 percent the soccer mom's fault. She blew through a blinking red light. The two drivers behind me had it on dashcam footage. But if I hadn't been drinking Patti's margaritas just beforehand, the whole thing might not have happened. Fortunately, I have enough power over my faculties that my possible impairment never entered the cops' minds.

I went back to Patti's. She let me in.

"Jesus, Dave, you look like shit. What happened?"

I went to sit on the same couch where, two hours previously, we'd been karaokeing to 1990s rap and sipping pink lemonade and tequila.

"This van came out of nowhere. I mean, like a comet or something. I didn't have enough time to stop and . . . Jesus, the woman driving it was covered in blood like the end of *Carrie*, and the two kids in the car seats in the back seat were stunned and making no noise at all."

"Wait—where was this? What corner?"

"Franklin and Covington."

"That intersection is a death trap. Sooner or later something had to happen."

"Well, it happened to me." I was fidgeting badly, the shock unraveling me. "Patti, get me a drink, okay?"

Patti is my brother's ex-wife. We always got along, and when she left Brent, I was on her side because Brent is a riptide who destroys everything that dares go near him. Patti thought she could change him. Seriously? People don't change. They decay. They adopt ridiculous beliefs to pretend they have control over a world that is utterly indifferent to them. But they don't change.

Once I had a drink in my hand, I told Patti about an accident I saw when I was really young in which an old-fashioned car, like from the 1970s, plowed into another 1970s car, and afterwards, both cars resembled balls of tinfoil covered in barbecue sauce. "It really fucked me up. I think I had PTSD or something like it for years afterwards. But in today's crash, that woman wasn't wearing a seatbelt—how is that even possible these days? The kids in the car seats looked like nothing had happened to them at all, but all the doors and panels and the roof of the van vaporized into confetti. Like they'd never existed."

"All these government safety regulations."

My phone buzzed. It was Joelle from the local police department. I picked it up and she told me that the soccer mom had just died.

"Holy fucking—"

"Dave, calm down," Patti said. "You're fine. You've been through a big trauma. Breathe. In, out, in, out, in, out."

"Get me another drink. Something strong."

"I don't know if that's the smart thing right now," Patti said.

"Please, just give me a drink, Patti."

"It might cloud your emotions."

"Cloud my emotions? Christ, I just want to be clubbed on the head and have all of this go away."

"Dave, you don't understand. I can't sit here and listen to you tell me that the crash might not have happened if you hadn't been drinking. It's my duty to let the authorities know the truth."

My blood froze. "The authorities?"

"I think that's why you and I have always been friends, Dave. We can see the truth when others can't."

I hadn't seen this coming. "Patti, you mean you'd narc me out?"

"Don't be so melodramatic. A woman was killed. Her children are motherless."

"She's dead and they're motherless because she drove into Covington Road without stopping at a blinking red light! That's why this happened."

"But you said it might not have happened if you hadn't been drinking."

"Patti, where is this coming from? The woman drove her car at right angles directly into a main traffic artery. They have footage from two dashcams to prove it."

"You were definitely over .08 and you know it."

"So fucking what? It wasn't my fault!"

"Or was it?"

"Patti, why are you going down this path?"

"This *path* is called my conscience, Dave, and I don't have any choice."

I went over to the cupboard where she kept her hard liquor. I opened it and poured myself a coffee mug of Stoli, swirled it around and chugged it. "You'd do that to me?"

"I'd also have to tell them that you chugged six ounces of Stoli right there."

"I have no idea who you are, Patti. You're about to ruin my life. My job. My benefits. My ability to travel out of the country on business. My ability to do just about anything. Once you have a DUI on your record, your life is burnt."

"I'd like to think you saw me as someone who had morals and valued truth."

"Seriously?"

"Yes, seriously. So drink a few glasses of water, gather your wits and let's go down to the cop shop together."

"Okay, you're right. I'm sorry. I don't know what came over me."

"The shock is what came over you."

"Yes, you really are right."

I walked over as if to give her a big hug, then grabbed her head and wrenched it around almost 360 degrees, killing her on the spot. How dare she be so preachy? I dragged her into the garage and lifted her body up into the cargo carrier on her car's roof. She'd be safe there for at least a short while until I figured out a next step.

Afghanistan does this to you.

60

Norovirus

I WAS ALWAYS THAT kid in class who was such a Fruit Loop that nobody, even the cruelest bullies, could be bothered to torment me. The teachers took pity on me and, during lunch hour, gave me the job of running the coffee machine and bussing tables in the staff room. I loved it because I didn't have to talk to other children. Instead, I'd collect used Styrofoam cups, check out the lipstick marks and raise my eyebrows at my teacher friend, Vice Principal Rathbone. I'd say something I'd stolen from *Hollywood Squares* or *Password*, along the lines of "Miss Clark's summery new shade of lipstick tells me she's left Mr. Right . . . and she's looking for Mr. Right *Now*."

Then she would ask me, "Erik, what happened in your life to make you so perceptive?" And it would be time to change the subject.

"Quick: why do bikers wear leather?"

"Why?"

"Because chiffon wrinkles." (I stole that line from Paul Lynde, RIP. I had to go to the library to learn what chiffon was, and it is a beautiful thing indeed, but also so very, very flammable.)

You'd be amazed at how easy it is to become cynical, or maybe you wouldn't. I think most people are cynical, but some don't realize that's what they've become. At least I actively went for it. An acid tongue was my shield. Lord, I can't even count the number of acid comments I've made to guys who could have been The One. But there I'd be, out in the parking lot, hyperventilating in my Camry, wishing I could have said something sugary instead. At least I owned a car back then.

I fondly remember my little Wedgwood-blue Rubbermaid elementary school bussing tray. I could pile any mess onto that tray and dump it: mess gone! I wanted my life to be a Rubbermaid bussing tray.

Sometimes even Mrs. Rathbone would try to be "real" with me and share some life advice, but I'd have none of it. "If you really cared about me, you'd help me get into one of those Fame schools where everyone's just like me."

"I think you need to be able to sing or dance to get into those, Erik."

"Nonsense. They just pretend everyone has talent. Fame schools are dumping grounds for freaks."

I stopped going to gym class when I was maybe nine. Instead, I went to the library. Once that became my secret deal with admin, I never hit another speed bump in that department. The other students assumed I was in someone else's gym class, and it was bliss.

For some reason, my school library had bound back issues of *Sunset* magazine, which was this 1970s magazine about middle-class Californian houses and people. I wanted to live inside that magazine, where it was always slightly above room temperature and guest bathrooms were covered in tasteful cedar slats and had squeaky-clean avocado-green fixtures. In my house, there was one bathroom shared with my four brothers that always smelled like puberty. No, wait, that's not true. It was worse. Especially in summer it could smell like a kitchen fridge in New Orleans three months after Hurricane Katrina, the ones Homeland Security wrapped in duct tape and spray-painted UNHOLY on the doors.

I realize this isn't even an actual story, with a beginning and end, I'm telling you here. It's bits of autobiography, but if our lives aren't stories, what are they? Glorified microbes on a petri dish? Funny, I look at the words "petri dish" and I'm reminded of one of my worst jobs ever, which was supervising entertainers on a Holland America cruise liner. We had a norovirus outbreak so severe that we had to berth in Panama City for two days. I didn't get sick but almost everyone else did, and it made me feel superhuman. But the ship did start reminding me of my childhood bathroom, even with the endless mistings of bleach and industrial decontaminants.

For everyone except me, working on a cruise liner was one massive fuckfest. Lord, anywhere and everywhere. They should have renamed that liner the *SS STD*. But all I could really do was look on. In my senior year of high school, I went from imp to blimp, and I have been overweight ever since. I've never made the sexual grade with others. You don't miss what you never had, I guess. That's a lie. I want sex as much as you or anyone else.

For the brief moments when people put me and sex together in the same thought, they usually pause for a long moment and then say something like "You know, Erik, you are loved." Not "I love you," but that passive, friendly, indifferent "you are loved." God, that makes me angry. But reality eventually registers, and I've given up hope that way. I've recalibrated my expectations from an endless willingness to settle for less and less and less to a cold willingness to settle for nothing at all. *Oh, boo-hoo, you dumb queen.*

I'd best finish up here by saying that the norovirus outbreak in Panama City did give me my first big break. When the ship's magician, Gerrard, got sent to Emerald Coast Urgent Care, there was a Hollywood moment where I had to ask "Is there anyone here who can do something/anything on a stage to shut people up for twenty minutes?" When I heard no reply, I borrowed a Cher circa 1976 wig from Stella, who ran the liner's gift shops and who was also in Emerald Coast Urgent Care. I became Trashe Blanche, and the rest is history.

Maybe you've heard of me. You *better* have heard of me, given how hard I've worked my ass off for forty years. I am what's called a workhorse queen. And fuck you, darling.

Since 1991, when he published his debut work of fiction, *Generation X*, DOUGLAS COUPLAND has written thirteen novels published in most languages. He has written and performed for England's Royal Shakespeare Company, is a columnist for *The Financial Times* of London and is a frequent contributor to *The New York Times*. In 2000 Coupland amplified his visual art production and has recently had two separate museum retrospectives, Everything is Anything is Anywhere is Everywhere at the Vancouver Art Gallery, The Royal Ontario Museum and the Museum of Contemporary Canadian Art, and Bit Rot at Rotterdam's Witte de With Center for Contemporary Art, and Munich's Villa Stuck. In 2015 and 2016 Coupland was artist in residence in the Paris Google Cultural Institute. In May 2018, his exhibition on ecology, Vortex, opened at the Vancouver Aquarium. Coupland is a member of the Royal Canadian Academy, an Officer of the Order of Canada, a Officer of the Order of British Columbia, a Chevalier de l'Ordre des Arts et des Lettres and a recipient of the Lieutenant Governor's Award for Literary Excellence.